ONE HUNDRED DESIRES

AN ASPEN COVE SMALL TOWN ROMANCE

KELLY COLLINS

BOOK NOOK PRESS

Copyright © 2023 by Kelley Maestas

No part of this publication may be reproduced, distributed, or transmitted in any form or by any means, including photocopying, recording, or other electronic or mechanical methods, without the prior written permission of the publisher, except as permitted by U.S. copyright law. For permission requests, contact kelly@authorkellycollins.com.

The story, all names, characters, and incidents portrayed in this production are fictitious. No identification with actual persons (living or deceased), places, buildings, and products is intended or should be inferred. All products or brand names are trademarks of their respective owners.

CHAPTER ONE

As soon as the seatbelt sign turned off, taller travelers rushed to grab their bags from the overhead compartments. Much smaller in stature, Vivian Armstrong had to stand on her seat to reach the carry-on she'd tucked in the bin above. Despite her efforts, the other passengers didn't notice her struggle.

Just then, a kind man from across the aisle offered to help. "Hey, kiddo. Do you need a hand?"

Vivian appreciated the gesture but politely declined. She was often mistaken for a child but was far from a youngster at thirty. "Thank you for your offer, but I'm good," she said with a smile.

The man chuckled. "Good things ... small packages, right?"

"That's what they say." Vivian wanted to say, "Oh, you have a small package? That's too bad," but she was used to the same over-used pleasantry and had stopped bristling at comments about her height long ago. She had often been overlooked and underestimated due to her more diminutive size. She had grown used to people's reactions when they first saw her; she always heard the same jokes about her being 'small but mighty' or 'bigger on the inside.' She had been told she was 'too short' to play sports, reach the grocery store's top shelf, and even ride certain rollercoasters.

Though she was five foot nothing, she refused to let her height limit her. Since she was a young girl, she had been determined to prove to the world that she could do anything anyone else could, especially anything her older brothers could do. She worked hard, paid attention to details, and was determined to succeed.

Vivian had also learned never to back down. She used her wit and humor to disarm people and never let them feel like their comments were taken too seriously. Instead, she laughed it off and used it to show her strength and resilience. With six brothers, there was no place in her life for weakness. It was survival of the fittest.

With determination in her eyes, she grabbed her bag, narrowly avoiding hitting the man next to her but proving she didn't need help. She felt a sense of pride and satisfaction as she stood tall and confident, ready to show the world just how powerful she could be.

As the line began to move, she swiftly exited the plane and was hit by the crisp afternoon air of April in Denver—a city that didn't know it was spring everywhere else. The cold seeped past her jacket and settled into her bones. Val, her brother, had booked her a car. She couldn't wait to hit the open road and start her adventure. However, when she arrived, she was surprised to find the parking lot of the national chain nearly empty.

A massive jet-black Yukon occupied spot N-47. The mere thought of driving it sent shivers down her spine. The last time she'd driven something that large, she needed a booster seat to see over the steering wheel and platform shoes to reach the pedals.

"This will never do." She marched to the customer service kiosk and waited for her turn. To her right, two children played with a jumbo-sized game of Jenga while Vivian waited for the man in front of her to negotiate a deal on a car.

Large blocks of wood tumbled to the ground, and the kids gave up and came to stand beside the man Vivian assumed was their dad.

When it was her turn, she walked to the desk, smiled, and said, "Reservation for Vivian Armstrong."

The woman behind the counter, whose name was Cassey, looked at her and smiled. "Your Yukon is ready. With your Elite membership, you don't have to wait in line. You get to grab and go. Unless you came for some snacks." Cassey pointed to a display that held everything that could give a person diabetes or a heart attack—all the good stuff like gummy worms, chocolate, and chips. Cassey moved from behind the counter and attempted to stack the wood blocks. "Whoever thought this was a good idea should have to clean up this mess after every customer."

Vivian kneeled and helped the woman pick up the blocks. "The Yukon is a problem for me." She wanted to murder her brother Val, who undoubtedly ordered it as a joke. She thought they were past the pranks, but now it appeared that wasn't true. "Do you have anything smaller?"

Cassey stood and went back behind the counter.

Vivian followed her and grabbed several treats for the road. It was a long drive, and one shouldn't travel into the mountains without supplies. She giggled as she picked out three candy bars, two bags of chips, and two packages of gummies.

Cassey's fingers danced over the keyboard. "I've got a Mini Cooper?"

"Seriously?" Vivian opened a candy bar and took a bite. Times like this required chocolate. She took another from the stand and placed it on the counter.

The woman shrugged. "There's a big Indigo concert in town. She hasn't performed since she gave birth, and it's a one-time gig. It sold out in less than an hour, and so did we. That band has a huge following."

Vivian looked at her weather app. There was a storm approaching, so she didn't have much choice. Mini Coopers weren't known for their handling in the snow, and she knew from living in New York that spring storms could bring lots of wet snow that turned to ice when the evening temperatures fell. "Fine, I'll take the Yukon." She glanced at the Jenga game. "Would you be unhappy if some of those pieces found a different home?"

"Take them all if you want." Cassey rang up the order and placed the snacks in a bag.

Vivian paid. "I just need a few." She picked up four and tucked them inside her bag. "What about tape? Do you have any I can buy, borrow, or steal?"

Cassey opened a drawer and lifted out a large roll of duct tape. "This is all I've got, but you can have it." She handed it over, and Vivian was on her way. Her life often required adaptations. Today would be a doozy.

It took her five minutes to adjust the seat and mirrors, and it still wasn't to her liking. She pulled a few things from her bag and stacked them on her seat before she taped the Jenga blocks to the bottom of her shoes.

ONE HUNDRED DESIRES

She texted Val.

> I'm on my way.

She waited a few seconds to see if he'd text back. As a professional bodyguard, she always prioritized safety and followed the rules behind the wheel. Stay alive, don't text and drive.

> We can't wait to see you.

She shifted uncomfortably on the clothes stacked beneath her bottom and even considered going back inside for more Jenga blocks but decided to make do with what she had.

> Be there in three hours. It had to be a Yukon, huh?

She waited for a response, her eyes fixated on the screen as the three dots danced, teasing her with anticipation before disappearing, only to reappear once more.

> I knew better than to get the Mini Cooper.

She set her phone down and headed off the lot toward Aspen Cove. This would be her first trip there since her brother left the business. Val invited her to the wedding, but she was on assignment in Rome and missed it. Today she was coming to meet the baby. Little Natalie Armstrong had entered the world only a few days ago, and although her mother was an award-winning actress, the baby was taking center stage. Once she got her fill of Auntie Viv time, she needed to clear things up with Val. He'd asked her to take over as the head of the company. It was an odd request since she was the youngest and had five older brothers who could step in to fill Val's shoes. She'd like to think it was because she was the most level-headed, and he considered her the best option. Still, deep inside, she knew it was because her name started with a V. She could almost hear him say, "You can't spell Vortex without a V at the beginning." The firm's name came from the boys' initials in the family. The V was for Valery, first for her father; when he passed, it was her brother. Next were Odin, Ramsey, Torren, Easton, and Xander. Without a V at the start, it was Ortex, which made no sense.

As she drove through the city, she kept her eyes on the mountain range ahead. She marveled at the stunning scenery before her when she got to the turnoff that guided her toward Mount Meeker. Towering peaks, lush forests, and sparkling streams passed by her window in a blur of green and blue and turned to white as she climbed to higher elevations. The winding road was steep and treacherous in places, but Vivian was an experienced driver and navigated it easily despite everything.

About an hour from town, she came across a man and a dog standing on the side of the highway next to a broken-down truck. She didn't usually stop for strangers. It wasn't wise, but she felt terrible for the dog. The temperature had dropped twenty degrees since she'd left Denver, so she pulled over and lowered her window.

"Do you need some help?"

"We could use a ride."

She glanced into the back of the SUV. She had the room. "I can take you as far as Aspen Cove."

"It's my lucky day, then. That's exactly where I'm headed."

"Climb on in." She unlocked the doors and waited for the man to get his shepherd situated in the back seat before he took the passenger's seat for himself.

She pointed to the bag on the console. "I don't have much to offer but gummy worms and chocolate. You're welcome to it."

"I appreciate the lift." He opened the bag and pulled out a candy bar. "And lunch. My truck petered out about an hour ago. Several people slowed down, but they kept going."

"What about your dog?"

He chuckled. "He's not a lover of sweets." He pointed to his rucksack. "I always carry his water and food. He's like my kid. He comes first."

She liked that he had priorities. She'd met a lot of selfish men who didn't consider others first. "Are you from Aspen Cove?" She reached into the Sour Patch Kid bag and took a handful. The first one always gave her the shudders, but the rest went down smoothly.

"No, but I've got friends there. Buddies from the army."

"Oh, it's nice to have friends." Viv thought about her life. Growing up with all brothers in a big family, she didn't need a lot of friends and had to be careful in choosing them. Her brothers were all handsome, and she found out early on that many of her "friends" were only there to get closer to the Armstrong boys.

"What about you?"

She grinned. "My brother just had a baby." She laughed. "I mean, his wife did. I'm an aunt."

"Exciting stuff. How long will you be in town?"

"Not too long, just until I get a new assignment." She'd be out of there when she got called to work. Small-town living might be great for her brother, but she appreciated things like 2:00 a.m. Taco Bell runs and all-night liquor stores. She'd almost bet her weapon that a Starbucks wouldn't be within an hour's drive.

"Military?"

"Nope." She sat taller. "Bodyguard."

He stared at her. "Seriously?"

She quickly took her eyes off the road to give him a once-over. He wasn't her type. He was too tall, too beefy. Men like him were born protectors, meaning they'd forever fight for dominance in a relationship. She liked strong men but with a soft side. Looking at him, she could see that army life had hardened him.

"Yep." She took one hand off the steering wheel and offered it to him to shake. "Vivian Armstrong, head of Vortex Security."

"I've heard of your company. I'm Jackson Knight." He glanced into the back seat at his dog, who'd been quiet since he came aboard. "That's Gunner."

"Nice to meet you, Jackson, and Gunner. You know, I almost joined the Marines."

He glanced at the rolled clothes and hawkeyed her makeshift platforms. "Didn't meet the requirements?"

"Actually, at five feet tall, I barely squeaked by. I considered joining because my family wouldn't allow me to participate in the family business."

"Why not?"

"Too small, too weak, too woman."

He laughed. "Have they ever seen a grenade? It's small but packs a punch. I've learned never to underestimate size, age, or gender." He held out his arm and flexed his muscle. "I got my ass handed to me arm wrestling a woman in Kandahar. She wasn't much bigger than you."

"It takes a real man to admit that. And in the end, I got them to change their minds. I proved I was worthy." She liked Jackson. He'd probably become a friend if she were staying in Aspen Cove.

"I learned long ago that I don't have to prove my worth to anyone but myself."

"I can't say I've learned that lesson yet," she said. "I find myself having to prove myself all the time."

"That's because people are idiots."

"That's something we can agree on."

He shifted in his seat to face her. "Tell me the most famous person you've protected."

She thought about the cast of characters contributing to her bank account over the years and realized she'd never been assigned any high-profile clients. Those always went to her brothers. "I'm more corporate than movie stars. My brother protected Cameron Madden, and now he's married to her."

"Wow. Would you marry a client?"

"Never. I have a strict code of conduct. Never mix business with pleasure."

"You're telling me if you were protecting someone like Jason Momoa, you wouldn't, you know … if the opportunity came up?"

"First of all, he's not my type."

"He's everyone's type. Hell, half the guys I know would bend their rules for him."

She laughed. "He's too big, too famous, and has too much hair for me."

"I got you." He reached back to give his dog a pat on the head. "There's a bar in town called Bishop's Brewhouse. It's owned by my buddy Bowie and his brother Cannon. That's where I'm headed."

"And I thought my family names were strange."

"I'd like to take you out for a drink."

Her foot slipped from the gas pedal to the brake, jolting them as the car slowed. "Sorry, umm…"

"It's not a date," he said. "It's a thank you for picking up a stranger. As I said, no one would stop."

"Have you looked at yourself lately? You're an intimidating figure." His head came within an inch of the roof, making him well over six feet tall. She could never date a man that tall and not have neck problems.

"You weren't afraid." He shrugged.

"That's because I can take care of myself. I'm a self-defense expert. And I snapped your picture with my phone and loaded it to the Cloud just in case."

"Well, I'm grateful."

She adjusted her ball cap and pulled at the collar of her black T-shirt. "Why aren't you asking me on a date?" She rarely dated, but it was usually a schedule conflict. Or maybe it was because no one asked. But why wasn't he interested?

"First of all, you're not sticking around. Second, you're not my type. I like my women—"

"Taller?" she asked.

He shook his head. "Nope, I'm an equal-opportunity man. I had a bad experience. I left my fiancée to go to war; she had a three-month-old when I returned. I was gone for a year. It's easy math. So, if I ever decided to go down that road again, I think I'd want a woman who only had eyes for me. Bodyguards have to be focused elsewhere."

"I'm sorry about that. People *are* idiots."

"It was painful but a blessing in disguise."

"You'll find the one. I hear they come at you like a freight train when you least expect it."

Vivian couldn't help but let out a slow whistle as she

drove down Main Street. "Is this it?" she asked, taking in the slim offerings of the small town.

There was a quaint diner, a charming bakery, and a humble corner store. The bar, with a sign that read "Bishop's Brewhouse," caught her eye, as did the nearby bait shop.

"It's enough."

In the scheme of things, it was probably all anyone needed as long as their expectations were low. "No Starbucks."

He chuckled. "You're going to save a fortune staying here."

She got to the end of town and circled the roundabout. In its center were a few benches and an open area where she could envision a giant Christmas tree for a town celebration. She'd been watching too many Hallmark movies. She pulled back down Main Street and parked before Bishop's Brewhouse. "Here you go. It was nice meeting you."

She stepped out of the SUV to stretch her legs but remembered her wooden blocks. After a few tugs, she tore them free and slid to the pavement. She first noticed the smell of something wonderfully rich and chocolatey.

Jackson let his dog out, and they rounded the car to say goodbye. "If you change your mind, I'll be here most evenings, helping my friends." He pointed to Bishop's Bait Shop. "I could be there too."

"Good to know." She lifted her nose into the air. "Something is calling me—something full of sugar and chocolate. Today is a no carbs left behind day." She patted Gunner on the back before returning to the vehicle to get her bag. Her mother had always taught her never to show up empty-handed. Technically, she wasn't, but she didn't know if an Amazon order of toys and clothes for the baby that arrived a day ago counted, so she followed the scent of home-baked goods down the street to B's Bakery. Did it belong to the Bishops too? If so, they had a monopoly on this town.

She opened the door and walked inside.

"Just a second," someone said from behind the counter. The door opened again, and another customer entered. A blonde head popped up from behind the counter. "Welcome to B's. I'm Katie. What can I get ya?"

CHAPTER TWO

Red Blakely and Griffen Taylor walked down Main Street, the crisp mountain air filling their lungs. The scent of pine trees and fresh snow mingled with the aroma of the nearby bakery. Aspen Cove was beautiful, but Red couldn't shake the trapped feeling. He longed for the freedom and excitement of the city, and tonight's show in Denver would be a welcome respite to his small-town hell.

As they approached B's Bakery, Red's eyes caught a glimpse of a petite woman slipping inside. She was shrouded in black as if trying to hide from the world. Intrigued, Red felt a magnetic pull drawing him to her. He nudged Griffen, motioning towards the door. "Let's grab a brownie before we head to the studio."

Inside, the warmth of the bakery enveloped him. The scent of freshly baked cookies and rich chocolate brownies filled Red's nostrils, making his mouth water. As they stood in line, he couldn't help but steal glances at the mysterious woman. He knew everyone in town, or at least they knew him. He was kind of notorious. Not Al Capone infamous, but Hugh Hefner, without the Playboy mansion, famous.

This woman seemed out of place, and Red wondered what her story was.

Katie popped up from behind the counter. "Welcome to B's. I'm Katie. What can I get ya?"

Red watched intently as the woman perused the offerings. "A dozen mixed brownies, please." Her voice was soft and sweet. The kind you'd hear from a kindergarten teacher when her class was behaving.

"You got it."

Katie took out a pink bakery box and lined it with waxed paper before placing several brownies inside.

Griffen leaned in and whispered, "Looks like you've found your latest muse, eh?"

Red smirked, his eyes never leaving the woman in front of him. "Maybe."

With a playful shove, Griffen sent Red stumbling forward right into the woman. The unexpected collision knocked her off balance, and they both tumbled to the floor in a heap.

"I'm so sorry," Red said, scrambling to his feet and offering her a hand. "I lost my balance and didn't see you there."

Her eyes flashed with anger, and she swatted his hand away. "You didn't see me? You were standing right there. It's not like I'm invisible."

He hated to call her a liar, but she was nearly unseeable. "You kind of are. All in black, you look like a cat burglar on a coffee break."

"And you sound like an ass." She turned back to face the counter.

"Are you okay?" Katie asked as she tucked a few more brownies inside the box.

The woman nodded. "I'm fine, but this guy must have a

brain injury. He's lost his mind if he thinks it's okay to comment on how a woman looks, let alone one he doesn't know."

Katie scowled at him and shook her head. "He's not known for his subtleness."

"He's never met me. This could be the best I've looked in a lifetime. Cat burglar? No, baby, I'm a ninja."

Griffen let out a laugh that could probably be heard in the storeroom of Bishop's Brewhouse.

Red's cheeks flushed with embarrassment, and he tried to recover. "I apologize. I didn't mean to offend you. I wasn't commenting on your looks. Behind the baseball cap, the hoodie, and the black jeans, I can hardly see enough to have an opinion." That was a lie. Her piercing green eyes caught his attention right away. "I'm Red, by the way."

She sighed, seemingly uninterested. "Viv. And just so you know, this isn't a good day. I've spent five hours on a plane and three in the SUV from hell. All I want are brownies and a bed."

"Red has one of those—a bed, I mean," Griffen chimed in. "And he's always willing to share it."

Red slugged his buddy in the arm. "Dude, shut up."

Viv narrowed her eyes. "If you two are some comedic team practicing your act on me, I'd advise you not to quit your day jobs, and maybe learn some manners. Your lives, let alone your beds, have got to be pretty empty with lines like that. Geez."

Katie rang her up, and after Viv paid, she walked past him like *he* was invisible. Red couldn't help but feel disappointed. She was different than his norm. She didn't know who he was and wasn't interested, which made her more intriguing. He'd spent his life being the prey to thousands of adoring predators. A quiver of excitement coursed through him at the thought of maybe being the one to do the chasing for once if she'd ever give him the time of day.

As Viv left the bakery, Red and Griffen exchanged awkward glances. Griffen rubbed his arm, his laughter dying down. "That went well."

Red's eyes lingered on the door where Viv had just exited. "Thanks for the shove, man. I was hoping to make a better first impression."

Griffen shrugged, a playful smirk still lingering on his lips. "Hey, at least she'll remember you, right? That's something."

"What will it be, boys?" Katie asked.

Red lifted two fingers. "Brownies, please."

Katie handed them their brownies, her expression a mix of amusement and sympathy. "She's new in town, visiting family, I think. Maybe you'll get another chance. It would be nice to see you settle down."

Griffen laughed. "Him, settle?" He rolled his eyes. "Oh, I mean, he settles all the time, but settle down? Not likely."

"There's more to life than one-night stands and an unlimited supply of penicillin from Doc," Katie said in her Texas twang.

She was joking about the antibiotics. He hadn't needed a dose since the band toured France eight years ago.

"Is someone spreading that rumor?" Red asked.

She smiled. "No, but I thought it was funny."

"Only if you're not on the receiving end."

She hung her head. "Sorry. It was in bad taste. I was following your lead. The brownies are on the house."

With the bag in hand, the two friends left the bakery. Red's mind was still on the encounter with Viv. Walking down the street, he couldn't shake the image of her emerald eyes and the fire that seemed to burn within them. He found himself hoping that their paths would cross again soon, and he'd have an opportunity to make amends and get to know her better.

The air had grown colder as the sun slid farther down the horizon, casting a soft golden glow over the snow-capped peaks. Red shivered, pulling his jacket tighter around him. Viv's words had gotten under his skin. They were colder and delivered more sting than the weather outside.

Red and Griffen arrived at the recording studio, the familiar sound of music and laughter greeting them as they entered. They ensured their equipment was packed and ready for the big show in Denver tonight. The atmosphere buzzed with anticipation and excitement as the rest of the band members prepared for the concert.

While they worked, Griffen couldn't resist teasing Red about his playboy behavior. "Today must have felt foreign to you. I've never known a woman to cross your path and not swoon. She looked at you as if you were nothing."

Red secured his bass in its case. Maybe that was what was bothering him. She didn't even look at him, she looked right through him as if he were unimportant, and he wasn't used to that. Deep down inside, he knew she was right. He was nothing. The women who clamored to be with him didn't climb into his bed because they loved or cared about him. They did it because he was famous. He was a notch on their proverbial belt. But take the spotlight away, and he was just a man—a simple man with little to offer. He pushed the feelings of self-loathing away and embraced his alter ego. "If she stays here long enough, she'll come around."

Samantha, known to the rest of the world as pop star

Indigo, walked past him. "One day, you'll find a woman who makes you want to stop your man-whoring ways."

He handed his instrument to the guy loading the van. "It's not like I'm hurting anyone. I don't sleep with every woman who asks, only the ones who ask nicely. Besides, I enjoy meeting new people."

Griffen chuckled. "Yeah, 'meeting new people.' I've seen how you 'meet' them, Red. But seriously, think about it. Maybe that encounter with Viv is a sign you should start looking for something more meaningful."

"Says the guy who asked for my playbook. When you settle down, you can talk to me about something meaningful." He paused, Viv's face flashing through his mind once again. He couldn't deny that there was something about her that fascinated him. "You could be right," he admitted, brushing a hand through his hair. "But I'm not ready to be domesticated." He looked at Dalton, Samantha's husband. "I hear the first thing they do is castrate you."

"Still got my balls and they're bigger than yours." Dalton tossed a folder at him, narrowly missing his head. When it landed, the pages outlining the setlist scattered on the ground. He caught a glimpse of the first song they'd play that night. It was "Echoes of Emptiness." It was like the universe was hitting him over the head with a sledgehammer today, or maybe it was pointing out the truth. People surrounded him, yet he always felt alone and empty.

Griffen clapped a hand on Red's shoulder, offering a supportive smile. "Take it one step at a time, man. Even neutered animals have a good life. Who knows, maybe Viv will show you there's more to life than just a string of casual encounters. As for me ... I'll keep my balls."

Red mulled over Griffen's words, wondering if maybe his

friend was right. Perhaps someone was willing to take him in. He was like a stray dog looking for a home. Sadly, it wouldn't be Viv's. If she was in town visiting family, she was temporary. He certainly wouldn't have enough time to change her mind about him. And he wasn't convinced he wanted to, but he'd be lying if he said the challenge didn't excite him.

As Red climbed into the waiting limousine, his mind wandered through the memories of his past relationships. Each one had started with such promise, full of passion and excitement, only to end in disaster. He couldn't help but feel a sinking sensation in his chest as he recalled the heartbreak, the arguments, and the eventual dissolution of each connection.

He was a crash-and-burn kind of man when it came to love, and he knew it. Somehow, he always managed to sabotage any chance of lasting happiness. Red had a knack for pushing people away just as things started to get serious. He found himself questioning if he even deserved to find love. Would he just end up hurting any woman he allowed into his heart? Did he have it in him to change, to break the pattern of destruction that seemed to follow him from one relationship to the next?

Griffen's voice broke through Red's thoughts, pulling him back to the present. "Hey, Red! You alright, man? You look like you're a million miles away."

Red shook his head, trying to dispel the gloomy thoughts that had taken hold. "Yeah, I'm fine. Just thinking about the concert and women."

"You never change."

That was a sad but actual fact. It was tough to teach an old dog new tricks, especially when the tricks he had up his sleeve were so rewarding, or at least had been in the past, but now he realized that even the most loyal dog got tired of savoring the same worn-out bone.

Hiding his internal turmoil, he went back to the persona everyone expected, Cocky Red. "Best not to mess with perfection."

Griffen chuckled. "I'm pretty sure your definition of perfection differs from most people's."

Red grinned. "That's why I'm special." As the limo pulled away from the studio, Red couldn't help but wonder if he was missing out on something more. He loved the thrill of the chase, the excitement of meeting someone new, but what if there was something deeper, something more meaningful out there? He sighed, pushing the thoughts away for now. He had a show to perform, fans to please, and music to make. But as he closed his eyes and leaned back in the seat, he couldn't shake the feeling that something was shifting inside him. Maybe, just maybe, it was time for a change.

CHAPTER THREE

The air was crisp and cool as Vivian made her way up the winding road toward her brother Val's lakeside home. She cracked the window and took a deep breath, savoring the scent of massive evergreen trees and moist earth that clung to everything here. The majestic mountains loomed over her. With each mile forward, Vivian felt like she was being absorbed by nature rather than encroaching on it.

She tensed up as she pulled into Val's driveway, her heart racing with anticipation. Before she could even step out of the car, Val came running out of the house like a giddy schoolboy and enveloped her in an embrace that felt like home.

"Viv! I'm so glad you made it!" His enthusiasm was infectious, and the nervousness she had felt moments ago evaporated in his strong arms.

"I wouldn't miss this for all the tea in China," she said, grinning so wide it felt like her face would split in two.

Her breath caught as they entered the house, and Vivian noted the breathtaking view of the lake from the living room windows. She spun around with stars in her eyes, clasping her hands together. "It's just ... wow!"

Val chuckled at Vivian's reaction to the cabin. "Yeah, it's pretty impressive, isn't it? Check out the fireplace. It's a work of art." He pointed to the wall on their left. "I hand-picked every single stone."

Vivian's eyes widened as she looked at the towering fireplace that dominated one entire wall, crafted with rough-hewn stones in various earthy tones. The flames danced and flickered in the hearth, casting a warm glow over the room.

"Take a seat. Cameron is changing the baby but will be out in a second." Val sat on an overstuffed leather loveseat while Viv was comfortable in the matching chair to his right. Her fingers ran over the soft cowhide that was the color of butter and felt just as supple and creamy.

Her attention was quickly diverted as Cameron entered, carrying Natalie in her arms. Vivian's heart skipped a beat at the sight of her sister-in-law, who was even more beautiful in person than in her countless award-winning films. Her stunning features were softened by the love and joy that radiated from her as she looked down at her daughter.

Vivian couldn't resist teasing her. "Well, now, she really is perfect! I'm so jealous!"

Cameron laughed. "Oh, she's not perfect. She's already had a few blowouts, and let's not talk about the every-two-hour feedings and sleepless nights. But she's worth it all."

"I was talking about you."

Her sister-in-law blushed, and her brother smiled. "I agree. I've got the perfect ladies in my life. Wife. Daughter. Sister."

Vivian leaned in for a closer look at the baby, taking in her tiny fingers, toes, and downy hair covering her head.

She couldn't believe how small and fragile she looked but how much joy she brought everyone around her. It was a new experience for Vivian, who had never been around babies.

Val shot Vivian a knowing look, mischief in his eyes. "Careful, Viv. You might catch baby fever."

Vivian waved him off with an exaggerated roll of her eyes. "Oh, please. Let's not get ahead of ourselves." But the truth was, she couldn't deny the warmth and joy filling her insides at the sight of Cameron holding their new bundle of joy. She could picture herself as an aunt, but motherhood? Was it possible? Could she overhaul her life and find a man who fit into the equation too? The idea sounded like more work than fun. She'd encountered two that very day—one who wanted to buy her a drink but wasn't interested in dating her, and one who had the sensibility of a tenth grader. There were no immediate prospects. She chuckled to herself.

Cameron kissed the baby's head and offered her to Viv. "Would you like to hold your niece?"

"I-I don't know if I should," she stuttered nervously, unsure of herself.

Cameron smiled reassuringly at her. "It's okay, Viv. Just hold her like this," she said as she demonstrated how to cradle the baby.

Vivian's hands trembled as she accepted the tiny bundle from Cameron. She supported the baby carefully, terrified of doing something wrong. Uncharacteristically, she felt as large and clumsy as an elephant beside Natalie's delicate and petite frame. She couldn't help but let out a nervous chuckle as she struggled to find a comfortable position for the baby.

Cameron smiled warmly at Vivian's nervousness. "It's

okay, Viv. She won't break. Just relax and enjoy holding her."

Vivian followed Cameron's advice and focused on Natalie's sweet little face. She marveled at how her tiny fingers curled around her own, and she couldn't help but let out a small coo of affection.

Suddenly, Natalie let out a loud, wet noise, and milk dribbled from the corner of the baby's mouth. Vivian's eyes widened in horror. "Oh no! What do I do? She's leaking."

Cameron laughed softly and reached over with a cloth to wipe the baby's mouth. "Don't worry, Viv. That's just a little gas. Here, let me show you how to burp her."

Cameron gently took Natalie back into her arms and showed Vivian how to pat her back before placing a burp cloth on Vivian's shoulder and handing her back. After a few moments, Natalie let out a satisfying burp, and both women sighed in relief.

Vivian couldn't help but feel a sense of pride and accomplishment at successfully burping the baby. She smiled down at Natalie, feeling a new sense of connection with the little girl.

Cameron grinned at Vivian. "You really are a natural. Are you sure you don't want to give Natalie a cousin?"

Vivian blushed at the suggestion but couldn't deny the warm feeling in her chest at the thought. "Nope, I'm happy being the best aunt ever."

"You're her only aunt," Val said.

Viv grinned. "Which makes me the best by default."

They all laughed, and Vivian settled back into the couch, cradling Natalie in her arms. She couldn't believe how much love she already felt for this bundle of joy.

"How was the drive?" Val asked.

Viv breathed deeply, hoping to capture the smell

forever inside her heart and mind. Natalie smelled like spring rain on new growth, like a breeze on a beach at sunset, like the bounce from a rubber ball, like buttercream icing melting in the sun. She pulled the baby closer to smell Natalie's sweetness—perfection.

"Drive was good. Picked up two hitchhikers." She watched her brother's brow furrow.

He pointed to Natalie. "She's not allowed to teach our daughter about stranger danger."

"It was fine. Besides, if he tried anything, I could have maimed him with the giant Jenga blocks I had to tape to my feet. And his dog was likelier to lick me than bite me to death."

Cameron cocked her head. "Wait...you taped Jenga pieces to your feet?"

Viv sighed. "Desperate times ... desperate measures, and all that." She pointed to Val. "He rented me a Yukon."

"Seriously?"

"She would have murdered me if I got the Mini Cooper. I was keeping our family intact."

"We could have sent a car," Cameron said.

"I like to drive. Even the Yukon was fun once I got myself situated." She stared down at her niece, who was shifting, moving, and rooting around for her next meal. "I think she's hungry."

Cameron sighed. "She's always hungry."

Val jumped up. "Speaking of hungry, I'm making dinner."

Viv laughed. "Beef or chicken ramen?"

Her brother looked like she'd offended him. "I'll have you know I've learned a thing or two living in the mountains. Unless I wanted to live off of Maisey's blue-plate specials or Dalton's take-and-bake pizza, I had to learn to cook." He stood and kissed Cameron.

"Wow, they can be trained," Viv joked as Val walked away to start dinner. She knew her brother could take care of himself and those around him, even if his cooking skills were lacking.

"So, what kind of dinner have you got in store for us tonight?" she called after him.

Val turned back and grinned. "You'll be impressed, I promise." He then disappeared into the kitchen.

"Can he cook, or should I get the box of brownies I picked up at B's Bakery from the SUV?"

"You bought brownies?"

"Yes. I was taught that you never go anywhere empty-handed."

Cameron clapped her hands in excitement. "You are my favorite sister-in-law."

"I'm your only sister-in-law."

"Right, but still my favorite."

Soon enough, Val emerged from the kitchen with a platter filled with salmon and steamed vegetables. As soon as the aroma hit Vivian's nose, her stomach growled loudly.

"Are you hungry?" Val asked.

"I ate on the way, but I could eat again."

Cameron rose and took the baby from Viv's arms, and they headed to the dining room table, where a large picture window overlooked the lake.

Val sat the platter down and narrowed his eyes. "I bet you already had fish today—Swedish gummy fish."

"No fish today, only worms."

"Speaking of worms," Val said with a smile. "Cameron is the only person who can outfish me with a baitless hook."

Viv let out a low whistle in admiration. "Did you catch these?"

Cameron shook her head. "No way! We got them at the store in Copper Creek. I wish we were that skilled, but all you'll catch in that pond is trout and a boot someone lost years ago."

As they began to eat, Vivian couldn't help but savor the flavors that burst in her mouth. The fresh herbs and spices perfectly complemented the delicate flavor of the fish. She closed her eyes momentarily, fully immersing herself in the experience.

When she opened her eyes, she took it all in. The sight of the lake lapping against the shore added to the serene ambiance of the cabin. Vivian's gaze was drawn to the sun starting to set, casting a warm, orange glow across the water. She understood why her brother gave up everything to be here.

Her thoughts drifted to the business aspect of her visit. She wondered when the best time would be to bring it up to Val, but she didn't want to spoil their peaceful moment with the baby and the delicious meal and decided to wait until they were more relaxed and settled in.

For now, she would enjoy her family's company and soak in the beauty of the place they called home.

CHAPTER FOUR

Red emerged from the dimly lit venue, his chest heaving with the adrenaline of the performance. The chilly night air sent a shiver down his spine, but he couldn't help but smile. Indigo had played an incredible set, and the crowd's roar still echoed in his ears. A high-pitched voice cut through the din as he approached the waiting limousine.

"Red! Over here!"

He turned to see a young woman, breathless and excited, running towards him. She had a shock of curly hair and a smattering of freckles across her nose. He could tell from her logo-emblazoned T-shirt and giddy demeanor that she was a fan.

She reached him, beaming from ear to ear. "Oh my God, Red, that was amazing! I sold my car for a ticket and hitchhiked from Cali to get here. I'm your number one fan, but you already know that. I'm Sarah, remember?"

Red squinted at her, trying to place her face, but he couldn't. After years of performing, the faces all looked the same. "Thanks, Sarah. I'm glad you enjoyed it."

Her eyes widened and then narrowed. "Don't tell me you don't remember me."

He wouldn't dream of it. The last time he didn't remember a fan, she showered him with a gin and tonic. "It's always great to see you."

The tightness in her expression seemed to soften. "Where are you playing next? I'd love to see you again."

Red shook his head. "This was just a one-night stan... I mean, show."

A cloud of sadness seemed to descend over Sarah's features, and Red felt a pang of guilt. He knew how much the fans loved Indigo's music and hated disappointing them. But he was also exhausted and just wanted to get back home.

"Let's take a picture." Her voice was tinged with desperation.

Red hesitated for a moment before finally relenting. "Okay, sure."

They posed for the photo, and Sarah leaned close to Red, her body pressing against his. He could smell the battle being waged between her drug-store perfume and the alcohol on her breath, with the alcohol winning, and Red felt a pang of sadness. Fans were almost always party girls, but he had never taken advantage of anyone drunker than him. He didn't have to; they were literally standing in line. He used to love these moments, the thrill of a one-night stand with a beautiful fan. The connection was fleeting but fun. Music and manifest desire. However, lately, he'd been feeling empty and unsatisfied. He'd been searching for something more meaningful than just sex, but he sabotaged himself each time he thought he found it. He'd ruined it with Cameron and with Deanna. The truth was, forever didn't exist in his world.

"I'm staying at a hotel nearby. Do you want to come over?" Sarah whispered in his ear.

Red's mind raced as he weighed his options. Sarah was undeniably attractive, and spending the night with her was tempting, but he was conflicted. They always wanted more, and he had nothing more to give. He realized he wasn't interested in Sarah's offer but didn't know how to let her down without hurting her feelings.

Before he could respond, Alex, their drummer, called out to him. "Red, we need to go."

He seized the opportunity to break away. "As lovely as that sounds, my ride is ready." He turned and walked away. Red felt a twinge of guilt as he climbed inside the stretch Samantha had ordered.

As he settled into his seat, he thought about the encounter with the red-headed cutie. He was glad he hadn't gone through with it but felt lonely. He wished he could find someone who understood his passion for music and his desire for something more profound than physical attraction. He knew it was a tall order.

The rumble of the engine filled his ears, and the cool leather of the seat against his back was a soothing sensation. The city's lights flashed outside the window, but Red was lost in thought.

"I'm surprised you didn't tie her to the roof," Dalton said. He and Samantha were inseparable.

"I'm over it."

"Not tonight," Gray said. His name was Gary, but he'd lost a bet with Red years ago and had to change his name to Gray legally. Red imagined he got laid a lot more without the weight of a name like Gary. The only good-looking Gary he could name was Cooper. He'd done the man a favor. "You'll be over nothing unless you find a fan hiding in your bed again."

"I'd hardly call it hiding." Last week he came home to a woman who had dipped herself in chocolate and was waiting for him. She'd ruined his 900 thread count sheets and caused him hours of paperwork. The town of Aspen Cove was fed up with his shenanigans, or that's what Sheriff Cooper said.

He couldn't control these women. What happened to the fans who only wanted an autograph or a photo? Nowadays, they want your baby and half your earnings. The creepy ones wanted a clipping of your hair—or worse—in a vial they hung around their neck. He'd never forget Paris, where he woke up bald. Some chick he'd invited back to his room brought a pair of clippers, shaved his head while he was passed out, and sold it on eBay. It only proved that he couldn't be trusted to make good choices. Not in women, at least.

He was torn by what he wanted and what he imagined the universe thought he deserved. He couldn't shake the feeling that he needed something more than just the fleeting encounters with fans and groupies. He had been living the rockstar lifestyle for decades, and it had lost its appeal. He wanted something real, something meaningful. Maybe he needed a dog. Then again, his last one ran away too.

The other members of the band were chatting and laughing, but Red was lost in his thoughts. He stared out the window, watching the city lights fade away as they headed back towards the small town in the Rockies where he lived.

Three hours later, the limo pulled up outside his house, and Red said goodbye to his bandmates. He was glad to be back in familiar surroundings. As much as he said he hated the town, it had become home.

He walked up the steps to his front door and unlocked it, stepping inside to the musty scent of old records mixed with the aroma of stale coffee.

Walking through the living room, he caught a glimpse of his first guitar sitting in the corner. It was still his favorite because his pops had bought it for him. He handed it to him for his tenth birthday. His old man called it a "gee-tar." The old instrument was a relic of a bygone era, with a weathered body and a cracked, yellowed finish that had seen better days. The wood had faded to a dark, almost black color, with the grain still visible beneath the wear and tear of years of use. The metal strings had lost their shine, and the tuning pegs were rusty and stiff. The fretboard had deep grooves worn into the wood from years of playing. The strings buzzed slightly when played, but the tone was warm and rich, with a depth that belied its age.

He picked it up and began to play, losing himself in the melody. As the music filled the room, he felt a sense of peace wash over him. This was what he needed. This was where he belonged. This was his love.

As he played, he thought about the encounter with Sarah. She was a good fan—the kind who was satisfied with a photo and a smile.

He knew he couldn't live like this, chasing temporary thrills and meaningless encounters. He resolved to focus on his music, to pour his heart and soul into every note. Red continued to play, the music filling the room and his soul. When his eyes drooped, he set the guitar back in the corner, brushed his teeth, and climbed into his empty bed.

Several hours later, the mattress shifted, and a deep sultry voice whispered in his ear, "It took me forever, lover, but I'm here." A hand snaked over his bare stomach and shifted south to what she had come for.

"What the hell?" Red bolted from the mattress and turned on the light. In his bed, wearing nothing but a smile, was Sarah.

"How did you get in here?"

"I used the code."

"You have my security code?"

"Everyone has it. It's posted on a fan site."

"What? What site?"

"Anything for Love, silly." She patted the space beside her. "Come back to bed." She glanced around the room and sighed. "I'm so glad nobody was here. That could have been ugly ... for them."

His heart pounded frantically as he watched the intruder lie back in bed as if she belonged. Angry and more than a bit scared, his mind raced, trying to devise a plan to get this person out of his room.

"You're trespassing," he spat out, his voice shaking.

He moved quickly, snatching his jeans from the chair in the corner and hurrying to put them on. But his movements were frantic and uncoordinated. The denim fabric felt stiff and rough against his skin, adding to his discomfort. He cursed as he struggled to get the pants over his hips. Despite his best efforts, the jeans seemed to fight back. He tugged at the fabric, pulling it up and then pushing it back down, trying to find the right position.

The intruder watched him, a smirk playing at the corners of her mouth. "Leave them off. It's more fun that way."

After what seemed like an eternity, he managed to get the jeans up and fastened. He turned to face Sarah and pointed to the door. "Get out," he said, his voice low and menacing.

"That's not what you want. You know it, and I know it."

"I'm calling the police." He picked his phone up from the dresser and dialed Aiden.

"Not again," Aiden answered.

"Sorry, Sheriff."

"I'm on my way."

"You should get dressed," he told her.

"I should, but I won't. I want you to see what you're missing."

Red turned around and left before she could show him more. He walked shirtless and shoeless into the icy cold night. He'd be lucky if he got anything less than frostbite, but it wouldn't be something he didn't deserve. He'd been reckless for years, and karma was returning to kick his ass.

Flashing lights lit up the night sky in the distance.

When the cruiser pulled into his driveway, Sheriff Cooper exited and approached. "Where is she, and what's this one's name?"

Red sighed. "She's in my bed, and her name is Sarah. I didn't invite her."

"Mmm hmm, sure." Aiden walked into the house but stopped and turned around. "I'm not your personal security team. This is the last time I use the town's resources to get you out of a mess. You need to hire someone." He disappeared and five minutes later came out with Sarah, who explained to Aiden that she would be Red's wife.

"He just hasn't adjusted to the idea yet," Sarah said.

Aiden walked her past Red and put her in the cruiser. "I'll be back, baby," she called from the cruiser's back seat.

He had no doubt that was the truth. Aiden's warning only added to his frustration. He resented the implication that he needed someone to protect him. But underneath his anger, he knew Aiden was right. He couldn't keep relying on the town's resources to bail him out of trouble. He needed to take responsibility for his actions and hire someone. The only bodyguard he knew was Valery Armstrong. Could he ask his ex-fiancée's husband for help? He was pretty sure Valery would rather hobble him than help him, but he was out of options.

CHAPTER FIVE

Vivian woke up refreshed and energized like she had slept for a week. She rubbed her eyes and stretched her arms, feeling the soft sheets of the comfortable bed beneath her. As she got up, she heard voices coming from the living room. Curiosity piqued, she quietly approached the door and pressed her ear against it. Val's voice rose and fell and blended in with the woodwork, but she took note of the other man's voice. She'd recognize that voice anywhere. Few men's voices ran through her veins like his did—deep and velvety, with a subtle rasp that sent shivers down her spine. It was a voice that commanded attention. She wanted to hate it, but she couldn't. It was a voice that spoke to her on a primal level, igniting a desire that she couldn't ignore.

Vivian hesitated for a moment, wondering if she should interrupt them or not. But her curiosity got the better of her, and she slowly pushed open the door and snuck down the hallway. When she peeked around the corner, she found her brother standing with his arms crossed and a scowl etched on his face as Red pleaded with him.

"I know you used to be a bodyguard, man. I need your

help," Red said, desperation in his voice. "It's out of control."

Val shook his head. "I'm sorry, Red. I can't help you."

"Why not?" Red asked, confused.

"Because you're a misogynistic, cheating asshole, who was once engaged to my wife," Val replied, his tone firm.

Vivian's eyes widened at the revelation. She had no idea that Cameron had been engaged before. Then again, she didn't know her sister-in-law well. But what were the chances that two ex-lovers would end up living in the small town of Aspen Cove?

Red looked taken aback by Val's words, but then he seemed to gather himself. "Look, I know I messed up in the past, but I'm trying to make amends. I need protection and don't know who else to turn to."

"What's going on?" Vivian stepped from the shadows into the room, interrupting their conversation.

"Nothing," Val said. "Go back to bed. Red was just leaving."

"Who are you?" Viv said. "My father?"

Red turned to face her. "This is who you're visiting? Val is your brother?" He let out a growl and shook his head. "Just my luck."

Val cocked his head to the side. "You two know each other?"

Viv shook her head while Red nodded.

"Is that a yes, or no?" Val demanded.

"We met at the bakery," Red said.

"It was more like he accosted me at the bakery."

Val grew with each step he took toward Red. "What did you do to my sister?"

Red stumbled backward. He held up his hands. "Nothing. I accidentally fell into her and knocked her down. No harm, no foul." He pointed to her. "Look, she's perfect."

She felt anything but perfect as she stood there in her flannel pajamas and hair tied up in a messy bun. Why hadn't she changed first? Oh, that's right, it was that damn voice that drew her like a moth to a flame. She needed more self-control, or she was destined to get burned.

"No need to protect me, big brother. I can handle myself." She turned to Red. "You were saying you need protection?"

"He was just leaving. We don't have anything to offer him." Val walked toward the door.

"You don't because you're no longer part of Vortex, but I might."

Red's brows lifted. "You work for Vortex?"

Viv smiled. "I'm in charge." She was supposed to be in charge, but by Val's behavior, it would seem like he thought he was still running things.

Val marched back into the room. "You're not working with him."

"As CEO, I choose our clients. You put me in charge for a reason."

"I did, but—"

"But nothing." She shooed him away with a wave, then turned back to face Red. "Now tell me about your problem."

"Last night, one of my fans broke into my house. She crept into my bedroom in the middle of the night."

"Fans? What am I missing here?"

Red smiled. "I'm a bass player for a band called Indigo."

Viv crossed her arms. "So, you're the reason I had to drive a Yukon." Yep, the man was trouble, all right. While he wasn't directly responsible for the rental car, he was indirectly involved, which made him an accomplice to her misery.

Red lifted his hands in the air. "I don't even know what that means, but I bet that was an interesting ride. Can you even reach the pedals? It seems like giving you a Yukon is the equivalent of giving a kid a ten-speed when all they are ready for is a tricycle."

Val laughed. "You're about to get a black eye." He started to walk away. "I'm checking on Cameron and the baby. Don't let any blood get on the carpet." He got to the hallway. "And don't forget. He isn't now and will never be a client of Vortex. He's an asshole, so stay clear."

"You're not the boss," Viv called after him, but he disappeared without another word, and she once again wondered why he put her in charge if he didn't think she could make sound decisions.

"I am an asshole," Red said. "But I have a problem, and I need help."

She turned in a circle to get her bearings in the strange house. "I can't tackle any problem without a cup of coffee. This may take two."

Red pointed towards the kitchen. "Looks like the coffee pot's over there." As she poured herself a cup of coffee, she couldn't help but think about what Val had said. She knew her brother was just looking out for her, but she also knew she had to make her own decisions.

"So, tell me more about this problem you have." Vivian sipped her coffee and sighed.

Red leaned against the counter, a serious look shadowing his features like a dark storm. "Like I said, last night, a woman broke into my house. She crept into my bedroom in the middle of the night."

Vivian's eyes widened. "If I recall correctly, your friend

said you have a bed you don't mind sharing. Is that not true?" She watched him squirm.

"Griffen was being a jerk."

"Okay. Did you report the woman to the police?"

Red nodded. "Yes, and Aiden, the sheriff, came out and removed her, but he told me he wouldn't spend another dime of the town's money to help me."

She took another sip and set her cup down. "You said a woman. Did you know her?"

Red rolled his eyes. "No. Yes." He let out an exasperated breath. "I don't remember her, but she remembers me."

"Is that a hazard of your job? So many women, so few morals? I mean memories?"

He kicked off the counter. "Look, either you're willing to help me or not."

She pointed to the chair across from her. "Have a seat, and we can discuss your needs."

"How many people work for Vortex?"

She leaned back and stared at him. The question was common, but something about it didn't sit right with her. It was like Red was interviewing her, but not for her services.

"Six, if you don't count my mother."

"She's a bodyguard?"

"No." The idea was laughable, but she controlled the giggle that threatened to escape. Her mother wielded a wicked spatula on Sunday mornings for pancake breakfast, but she'd never fired a gun, been in a fistfight, or driven in a high-speed chase. "Let's talk about what you need. I'm a bodyguard, not a mind reader."

Red looked at her skeptically. "You're not exactly built like a bodyguard."

Vivian stiffened, but she tried not to show it. "That's because the word bodyguard conjures images of big unskilled men. I'm skilled, smart, and strong. I'm an experienced personal security expert. I can handle myself, and I can handle you or anyone slithering into your bed uninvited."

He shook his head. "Maybe, but it's hard to take you seriously when you're sitting there wearing..." He leaned closer to take in the print on her pajamas. "SpongeBob."

She leaned back with her coffee in her hand. "What do you wear to bed?" She raised her cup to her lips and took a drink.

He gave her a crooked smile. "Nothing."

She nearly choked. Not because he wore nothing to bed but because she could almost envision what that looked like. *Lucky little stalker.* She shook her head and set her cup down before she dropped it.

"So, when this woman came into your room last night, you were wearing nothing?" His brows lifted as she took in his tight-fitting gray T-shirt that hugged his pecs like a lover. She closed her eyes and tried to banish the image she'd created. What the hell was she doing? This was the annoying asshole who dismissed her in the bakery like she was a pesky child. "Never mind. It's irrelevant."

"To you. You didn't get a reach-around at three this morning."

No, she didn't. It had been a long time since she'd gotten anything from anyone at three in the morning. The last real action she'd seen between the sheets was when she was on assignment in Australia and woke to find a snake in her bed. At first, she thought it was a lover's caress until she came to enough to remember she didn't have a lover. She flung that snake across the room and watched it slither out the open sliding glass door. "It sounds like this isn't unusual for you if the sheriff tells you to stop calling him."

"It's a problem."

"Get a security system."

He closed his eyes and sighed. "I have one. Sarah got the code from some website."

"So, you do know her." She'd never had the opportunity to protect anyone like a rock star, but she knew they had reputations. A girl or ten at every venue wasn't uncommon. Her brothers had worked for many musicians, mafia dons, and movie stars. She always got the babysitting duty. Not cute infants like her niece but entitled teens, tweens, and college-age beauty queens. They gave her jobs like getting high-profile kids to college or spring break details which made her the big meanie when she wouldn't let them drink until their livers exploded or have orgies in their presidential suites that daddy or mommy paid for.

"I don't remember her."

"That makes you an asshole." His voice might be sexy, and his body a wonder to behold, but his attitude toward women was a character defect, and she didn't do assholes. That made this the perfect job for her. It was a job where she could prove herself once and for all to Val and show him that his trust was not misplaced. She could do anything her brothers could. Besides, Red had fan trouble because he hadn't established the rules. That was one of her strengths. All it would take was tweaking his current security protocol, getting a new system, and training his overzealous fans. That was something she could do with her eyes closed.

"I charge a hundred dollars an hour."

He seemed to shudder for a second. "That's twenty-four hundred a day."

"Do you think you'll need around-the-clock protection? It's not like someone has threatened your life. You've got a security breach that is easy to fix. Let's start there and see what happens."

"Okay, who will you send?"

Vivian smiled, feeling more confident with every passing moment. "You get me. Just tell me where and when to meet you later today."

"You? I'm not sure you can handle this job."

Vivian felt a flash of irritation at his comment. "Really? Depends on what you think the job is. I can handle fists and guns as well as anyone, but they are of little use in private protection. Fists and guns are the last line of defense. A strong security protocol means we rarely or never have to use them. I can handle anything you throw at me, but it seems to me you're doubting my ability to protect you."

"I'm sure you're really great at what you specialize in, but..."

She laughed and then smiled. "I get it. You need proof that I can deliver on the fists. How about this. Let's arm wrestle."

"You think you can beat me?" He raised his arm and flexed.

"I don't know but we'll soon find out. If I win, you hire me for the job. If you win, I'll help you find someone else."

Red raised an eyebrow, seeming amused. "You're on. But I should warn you, years of playing the bass have built up these guns." He flexed them again as if that would intimidate or change her mind.

Vivian grinned, feeling a sense of excitement. "I'm not afraid of competition." The adrenaline pumped through her veins. They locked hands and counted down from three, each straining against the other's grip.

Despite his impressive biceps, Red's face contorted with effort as Vivian held her own. She'd been arm-wrestling her brothers her whole life and knew all the tricks, from body alignment to that slight bend of her wrist that puts an opponent at a disadvantage. Slowly but surely, she gained the upper hand, and in a sudden burst of strength, Viv slammed Red's hand onto the table, grinning triumphantly. "Looks like I got the job," she said, feeling satisfied.

Red chuckled, seeming impressed. "I guess you do. I must admit, I didn't think you had it in you."

"Don't let the package fool ya. Didn't you hear me say I was a ninja?"

Red nodded, seeming to take her seriously now. "Alright. I'll send you the details of where and when to meet me later." Red rose and walked out the door.

A few moments later, her brother walked into the kitchen. "Finally gave him the boot?"

"No, he's my next client."

Val's face turned radish red. "I told you, he's an ass—"

"Yep, he is. That seems to be the case for many of our clients. I don't care about their attitude. I only care about the job."

"You can't do this job."

Vivian bristled at her brother's words. "Excuse me? Who's in charge of Vortex now? Can't do the job? I expect that from asshole strangers, but you?"

Val looked at her sternly. "I am still your older brother, Viv, and I'm telling you, you can't take this job. You're not ready for it."

Vivian's eyes narrowed with frustration. "I've been training for this my entire life. I'm more than capable of handling any job that comes my way."

Val shook his head. "This isn't a game, Viv. You're not just dealing with a senator's kid who wants to go to the

Hamptons for summer break. This guy is the worst kind of man. He's a player and a cheat. You're not ready for him."

"I'm not dating him or sleeping with him. I'm going to check out his security system, make suggestions and develop a protocol. It's a simple job." She was so angry her ears burned. "I'm more than capable."

Val sighed, seeming torn. "Viv, please."

"Did you or did you not put me in charge?"

"I did."

"But it wasn't because you thought I could do the job?"

He shook his head, and she wondered if that was his answer. Then he scrubbed his face with his palm. "It was a logical choice. You were the only one without a specialty."

"Not true. I did all the cyber security and babysitting details." She gasped. "You gave me the shit jobs because you didn't think I could handle anything else."

"That's not true, but Viv, look at you. You're five foot nothing. A strong wind could pick you up in a storm."

She rose and put her cup in the sink. "I'm so glad you have so much confidence in me. I bet you only put me in charge because I'm great at scheduling, and my name starts with a V. You can't spell Vortex without one." She marched toward the hall but stopped. "You think Red is bad? Look in the mirror."

When she turned around, Cameron was standing there holding the baby. "What did I miss?"

"Just a sibling squabble." Viv stopped to kiss her niece on the head. "I accepted a job for Red Blakely. I believe you used to be engaged to him."

Cameron's eyes got big. "How did you know?"

She didn't want to say that she'd been eavesdropping. "It came up. What do you really think of him?" She waited for Cameron to tell her the same thing Val did, that he was a despicable human being.

Cameron's lips pursed before they relaxed with a sigh. "I have mixed feelings about Red. I loved and hated him, but I don't think I fully understood him. I don't think he's a bad man, but I don't think he knows anything about love."

It wasn't Viv's job to school him on love, but she could teach him how to protect himself, and that paid a hundred bucks an hour.

CHAPTER SIX

Red eyed his quaint Victorian house, trying to imagine Viv's reaction. Would she find it charming or rustic? He surveyed the front yard and knew she'd have complaints. It lacked the necessary security gate. Instead, there was a white picket fence with an open invitation for anyone to simply waltz in and hide under the shrubbery, which he had caught more than one surprise intruder doing in the past month.

Red smirked. His house wasn't exactly Buckingham Palace, but not a flophouse either. He stepped toward the vibrant red front door. It added a pop of color and gave him a way to insinuate himself into the architecture.

Red grabbed the doorknob and inhaled deeply as he walked inside. It still smelled like stale coffee, old records, and dirty socks. She thought he was an asshole which was fine. He didn't want her to think he was a slob as well, so he picked up everything that was out of place and opened all of the windows to let in a gentle breeze.

As he walked, his feet creaked on the wooden floors. He couldn't help but snicker, reminiscing about how he'd pestered the Cooper Construction boys to make sure his house had an antique vibe despite being a kit-build and as new as could be. Kudos to Owen, Ian, and Paxton for constructing a residence in Aspen Cove that appeared to have been around since the time of its first settlers.

There was a knock on the door, and he took a deep breath before opening it. On the step stood Viv. Gone were the comfy pajamas; now she was clad in full security-guard regalia—blue jeans, Vortex logo polo shirt, and most surprising of all, steel-toed army boots that could turn any shin bone to dust. She wore her confidence like a crown and held her clipboard close to her chest like a shield.

"Ready to get started?"

"Yeah, come on in." He stood back and let her inside.

Viv began to inspect every nook and cranny of Red's home, making notes on her clipboard as she went along. It was like Viv was a chemist examining a new substance. Every now and then, Red saw Viv's lips curl up into a wry smile as she pointed out yet another flaw with the system.

"Your security system isn't great," she said, shaking her head. "There are gaps in your defense bigger than the Grand Canyon."

"I know it's not good if all someone has to do is look on a site called Anything for Love to get my code."

"What is your code?"

He hesitated a moment. "58008."

She turned and gave him a wry look. "Seriously. What are you? Ten?" The fact that his code spelled BOOBS on an upside-down calculator shouldn't surprise her. She should have expected it. He'd bet that she'd seen everything from hoes to gigolos over the years given her line of work.

"Your system sucks." She moved to the entry where the floor creaked. "This is the best thing you've got right now.

This creak will let you know they're in, but then it's too late."

Red felt a pang of disappointment at her words, but he knew she was right. "What do you suggest?" he asked, hoping she would have some ideas.

Viv gave him a small smirk. "I'd suggest an entire overhaul of the security system here. I'd start with some state-of-the-art motion sensors and a robust surveillance camera system." She walked onto the porch and gestured towards the cameras he had mounted. "One has gum stuck right there on the lens, and the other appears to be hosting its own wasp hotel. Do you ever bother checking out the live stream?"

"Live stream? I have a live stream?"

She sighed. "You are going to be a huge project."

"In other words, you're going to charge me a fortune."

She walked past him and back into the house, tapping his shoulder with her pencil. "Exactly—if I agree to continue. Your safety has to be as much a priority for you as it is for me."

Red nodded, impressed by her expertise, and entertained by her personality. "Okay. Just tell me what to do."

She laughed. "Oh, I will. That's my favorite part of this job."

Viv looked around thoughtfully before turning to him. "You also need a new lock. I can pick this with a paperclip and a credit card."

"Seriously?"

She nodded. "Watch me." She locked the door and walked outside and less than two minutes later she was standing in front of him. "You're getting a dead bolt."

Red nodded, feeling a sense of embarrassment. He had

always thought his door lock was secure, but Viv proved otherwise.

As they continued to walk around the house, Viv pointed out several other areas that needed improvement. Red felt a sense of gratitude and relief that Viv was there to help him, even though it stung his pride to realize how vulnerable he'd been.

After an hour, Viv had finished her inspection and was ready to leave. Red felt a sense of disappointment that their time together was over, but he knew that she had given him a lot to think about.

"Thanks, Viv," he said, walking her to the door. "I appreciate your help."

Viv turned to him, giving him a small smile. "No problem, Red. Just doing my job."

Red watched as she walked down the steps and got into her SUV. He couldn't deny the attraction he felt for her, even though he knew she was strictly professional.

When she left, he closed the windows and locked up his house to the best of his ability and headed to Bishop's Brewhouse where he found Doc sitting at the bar by himself. He'd watched just about everyone in town play and lose tic-tac-toe to Doc. He'd heard a million times that it wasn't about the game, it was about the wisdom that Doc imparted on people while they shared a beer. He'd never been brave enough until that moment.

He slid into the stool beside Doc. Not knowing what to do, he simply sat there and stared at the mirrored wall across from him.

"Are you buying or playing?"

Red turned to face the old, grizzled man. If Wilford Brimley and Tom Selleck had conceived a child together, it would have been Doc Parker.

"Does anyone ever win?"

"No."

"Then I'll pay."

Cannon strolled in from the back room with a guy Red didn't know following close behind him. The man stepped forward. "I'm Jackson. What can I get you?"

Red pointed to Doc's almost-empty mug. "He'll have another, and I'll have the same."

Cannon's eyes grew saucer large. "Pull the beers and disappear. This is a mentoring session, and that guy might be here all night if Doc is feeling chatty."

Red pulled a twenty from his pocket. "I'm not playing, I'm paying."

Cannon laughed. "That's the first smart thing I've seen you do."

Jackson poured the beers and followed Cannon down the hallway. Doc took a sip and out of the corner of his eye, Red saw him lap the foam from his mustache.

"Tell me, son. What's on your mind?"

He had lots on his mind. Like the cost of a new security system and why a woman he wouldn't have given a second glance two weeks ago now piqued his interest, but those were problems for another day.

"Do you think some people are just destined to spend their lives alone?"

Doc Parker leaned back in his chair and stroked his bushy white mustache. "Well now, that's a mighty big question. But let me ask you this. Have you ever seen a rose bush that didn't bloom?"

"Only if it was dead."

"You ain't dead, son. So, I ask again with more clarity. Have you ever seen a live rose bush that didn't have the potential to bloom?"

Red shook his head. "No, I don't think so."

"That's right," Doc Parker said with a twinkle in his eye. "Even a scraggly rose bush can bloom into something beautiful if it's given enough care and attention. The same goes for people, son. We all have the potential for love and happiness, but sometimes we need help getting there."

Red nodded thoughtfully. "I guess you're right. But sometimes it feels like I'm just not meant to find love."

"Rumor has it that you get a lot of love."

He leaned in close enough to smell Doc's Old Spice aftershave. "That isn't love." It brought him right back to his childhood, watching his father slap it on his face right before he left for the bar. Those nights, which were many, Red spent alone eating Hungry Man TV dinners and watching reruns if they had power.

"I'm glad you recognize that." Doc Parker chuckled. "Son, love ain't something you find. It's something you create. You gotta put in the work, tend to it like a garden, and let it grow. And sometimes, you gotta be willing to take a risk and put yourself out there, even if it means getting hurt." He turned to face him and lifted a single winged brow. "You put yourself out there a lot, but you're not really offering anything of value." Doc poked him in the chest right at his heart.

Red nodded again, feeling a sense of understanding. "Thanks, Doc. I appreciate your wisdom."

Doc Parker emptied his beer, stood up, and patted him on the shoulder. "Anytime, son. And remember, the world has plenty of weeds and thorns to make us think twice about our roses. If a determined gardener can't be beaten by those pesky thorns, why should you settle for anything less than your perfect bloom?" He glanced at his watch. "Lovey is waiting for me."

"Is she the rose or the thorn?"

He looked at his watch. "Depends on if I'm late for Dancing With the Stars."

As Red watched Doc Parker disappear, a thought hung in the air. If a gardener can take care of their garden and never give up on their roses, why couldn't he do the same with love?

CHAPTER SEVEN

As Viv parked her car in front of Val's cabin, the sun was beginning to set, casting a warm golden glow across the landscape. She noticed movement down by the water and made her way towards the edge of the lake.

As she got closer, she realized that it was a family of elk, drinking water from the lake's edge. She watched in awe as the majestic animals moved about, the buck's antlers glinting in the fading sunlight. He caught her movement and stilled as if waiting to see if she was friend or foe. The largest female herded the littler ones together and they both stood guard.

As she watched the elk, she realized how protected she'd felt as a kid. No wonder she went into the protection business. There was great satisfaction in knowing that she could provide comfort for someone else. She thought of Val and Cameron and how they would forever protect Natalie. Val was the buck and Cameron the protective doe. Both of them were formidable.

Shaking off her musings, Viv made her way up to the

cabin and walked inside, finding Val standing in the hallway, scowling.

"Hello to you too. What's wrong?" Viv asked, sensing his irritation.

"I told you not to work with Red and you did it anyway." Val stepped aside to let her in. "He's bad news, Viv. I don't want you getting involved with him in any way."

Viv rolled her eyes. "He is a client like any other. He needs my help. I'm a private protection and security expert. Remember? That's what Vortex does. And we're damn good at it. His security system is a mess, and he's willing to pay top dollar for me to fix it. Besides, it's not like I'm getting involved with him personally. It's a job that puts money into the Vortex coffers. That is one of the main responsibilities I have as CEO. I don't know what you're afraid of, Val. You got the girl and then some. You won. Red is no threat to you or your family. I don't have a beef with him. He's a jerk, but that doesn't mean he should wake up to stalkers grabbing his crotch in the middle of the night. You know as well as I do how these threats can escalate."

Val huffed while Cameron came out of the kitchen, holding the baby. "Hey, girl! How was your day?"

"It was good," Viv replied, returning Cameron's smile. "I spent the afternoon with Red, helping him with his security system."

Cameron's smile faltered slightly. "How is Red?"

Her brother grumbled something about leopards never changing their spots and took a seat on the sofa.

She knew she was fighting an uphill battle. "Yes, I'm sure that's true, but it's good money for Vortex Security, spots and all. Besides, it's the right thing to do. He's not the first client with a history, you know." She took the overstuffed chair beside him and sat. "Let's just get to the bottom of this now. Am I really running the company or is this misplaced loyalty to our parents' naming conventions?" She needed to hear him say that he thought she was capable. Once he did then everything would be all right in her world.

"Look, Viv, you're a badass and fully capable of doing anything you set your mind to do. But keep in mind that I made a promise to Dad before he passed to protect you. I can't do that sitting in a remote cabin by a lake while you're shifting from city to city as a bodyguard for who knows who."

Her hackles rose. "Oh, so because you decided to retire, that means I have to sit behind a desk. That wasn't your job before. I thought I was taking over for you which meant I'd get better jobs—jobs like you used to do."

"The boys can take care of the tough stuff. You don't need to."

Cameron walked in and took a seat with the baby. "Are you telling her that she's not capable because she's a woman?"

"No, I'm not saying that but look at her. She's—"

"She's what?" Cameron asked.

Viv loved that her sister-in-law was coming to her defense.

"I'm not big enough, strong enough, or mean enough," Viv said.

Val waved his hand in the air. "Oh, you're mean enough." He rubbed his jaw and frowned. "I'm confused. Are we talking about supporting Red's needs or running Vortex?"

Viv sighed. "They aren't exclusive of one another. If you don't think I can handle the job with Red, and it's a simple security protocol revamp, then you can't possibly believe I'm capable of stepping into the role of CEO of Vortex. If that's the case, why did you put me there?" She stared at Val, who looked like a mouse trapped by a cat.

Val shifted in his seat. "It's not about you being a woman, Viv. It's about Red. I don't trust him, and I don't want you getting involved with him. He's trouble."

Viv shook her head, frustration building within her. "You're being ridiculous. Whatever problems Red has with you and Cameron are your issues, not mine. He's been nothing but appreciative and professional if you leave out the light jabs about my height. Red needs our help, and I'm the best person for the job."

Val stood up, towering over her. "I don't care, Viv. I don't want you working with him. End of discussion."

Viv clenched her fists, her temper starting to flare. "Whoa, cowboy! You think just because you built a cabin and moved to the country you can wrangle me? You can't tell me what to do today any more than you ever could, Val. I'm a grown woman, and I can make my own decisions. Frankly, right now I'm trying to decide if I should put your fears to rest and just knock you down like I did more than once during our years of training. You know I'm capable. If you can't trust me to handle this relatively simple job because you have an issue with the client, then I can't imagine how you expect me to run Vortex at all." With that, she stormed out of the cabin, slamming the door behind her.

She drove back into town practically shaking with a mix of anger and frustration. She couldn't believe Val was so stubborn, so unable to see things from her point of view. Then again, he was doing what he always did. He was trying to protect her but that's not what she needed. She was looking for validation and support. Why did it always come to this? She shouldn't have to prove or justify herself over and over to the people who know her best and damn well know all of her strengths.

Needing to blow off some steam, she headed to Bishop's Brewhouse and as she walked inside, she spotted Jackson behind the bar, tending to the customers. He looked up and smiled as he saw her, waving her over.

"Viv! You changed your mind. Can I buy you that beer?" he asked, wiping down the counter.

She took a seat at the bar. "Just needed to get out of the house for a bit. I'd love a beer."

As she looked around the bar, she spotted Red sitting at the end, nursing a tall draught. She debated whether or not to approach him but decided that she might as well say hello. It would seem unfriendly and awkward just to ignore a client.

"Hey, Red." She gave him a nod and shifted down to take the stool beside him. "Is this seat taken?"

Red looked up. "I thought you were headed home."

Viv nodded. "I changed my mind and decided to see what Aspen Cove has to offer."

"Or you got back, and Val read you the riot act for helping me," Red said.

"Something like that."

Red picked up his mug and took a drink. "Look, I can't blame him. You're his baby sister and I don't have a squeaky-clean reputation in this town. Then there's the fact that I was briefly engaged to your brother's wife, and I did her wrong."

"Did you ever apologize?"

He stared straight ahead for a few seconds and then turned to look at her. "I did."

She smiled. "That must be why she's more forgiving."

His eyes widened. "You think she forgives me?"

"Well, I don't know what you did, but she told me she has loved and hated you but mostly she doesn't understand you."

"I don't understand myself most days."

Jackson walked up and set a frothy cold ale in front of her. "You didn't say light or dark, so I chose for you. If you don't like it, I'll give you another."

She stared down at the dark beer and smiled. "You got it right."

"I would have taken you for a light beer girl," Red said.

"You also didn't think I could beat you in an arm-wrestling battle."

Jackson laughed. "Don't mess with G here, she'll destroy you."

"G?" Red asked.

Viv had no idea what Jackson was talking about, so she shrugged and sipped her beer. The cool fizziness went down easy.

"Grenade. She can fit in your pocket but pack a powerful punch."

"I can already see that about her." He rubbed his arm. "And I'm not too much of a man to admit she handed me my ass this morning."

Viv set her mug down. "I cheated." She laughed when Red's mouth dropped open. "It's almost never about strength and always about how you position yourself."

"Did she get closer and twist your wrist?" Jackson asked.

Red nodded.

Jackson laughed. "That means she had the upper hand from the beginning."

Red seemed to ponder that for a moment. "I wouldn't

call that cheating. I'd call it using what you know to your advantage."

"I like that you're not offended." Viv picked up her glass and tapped his. "Here's to men who don't need to flaunt their brawn to compensate for a lack of brains."

"I'm not sure if that's a compliment or not," Jackson said.

"It isn't." Red added, "But it's not too far from the truth."

The door opened and in walked a few women. When Red looked over his shoulder, he groaned.

"Someone you know?" Viv asked.

"The one with the red hair is why I need you."

Viv looked at the women's reflection in the bar mirror. They weren't dressed for the impending storm. They were dressed for a nightclub. Viv guessed that if this was the only bar in town, then it probably served as many things including the pick-up place.

From their conversation, she deduced that the red-headed woman was Red's stalker, and she was headed straight their way. "Red, you were a naughty boy, and I'm going to make you pay for having that sheriff pick me up. But I promise you'll love every minute of it." She raked her hands through his hair and was getting ready to accost him with a kiss.

Viv locked eyes with Red, feeling the tension between them. Before the woman could reach his lips, Viv pounced forward and captured his mouth in an electrifying kiss. Red's body was rigid at first, as if he'd been petrified by her sudden move. However, Viv felt his surprise dissipate into a tender caress as she moved her hands up to cradle his face and explored every inch of his mouth with a desire so intense it took her breath away.

Sarah pulled back, clearly taken aback by Viv's sudden move. Viv felt a mix of exhilaration and embarrassment. She had crossed a line, and she knew it. But at the same time, she couldn't deny the rush she felt from kissing Red.

He looked at her, a mixture of surprise and amusement on his face. "Well, well, well. Looks like someone's feeling possessive."

Jackson laughed. "So that's your type. Hmmm, I wouldn't have guessed that." He walked away, shaking his head.

"Who the hell is she?" Sarah stood with fists on her hips.

"I'm the reason you're going to turn around and leave." Viv made a move to get up, but the woman shook her head and retreated to the table where her friends sat.

Viv blushed, feeling embarrassed by her actions. "I'm sorry, Red. I shouldn't have done that. It's just ... I don't like the way she was talking to you."

Red grinned, clearly enjoying the attention. "No need to apologize. I kind of liked it." He shook his head. "Not her but you."

Viv rolled her eyes, feeling a smile tug at the corners of her lips. "You're impossible."

"So I've been told."

She took a drink of her beer. "Just to be clear, I was running interference. That kiss meant nothing."

He grinned. "That's the first time in my life that nothing felt like something."

It was something all right. It was a huge mistake and Red was trouble with a capital T.

CHAPTER EIGHT

Red sat there savoring that kiss for several minutes. He didn't even want to drink his beer for fear that it would wipe away her taste from his lips, but he couldn't waste a good beer, so he drank deeply, hoping to move the essence of her deeper inside. Only after the last drop did he allow himself to truly savor the kiss, the taste of her lips, the warmth of her skin, the softness of her touch, and the moment still lingering in the air around him.

He sighed and took a deep breath, realizing the moment had gone. But he still felt a warmth inside that was new and an ache for more. He wanted to reach out and touch her again but thought it unwise. One look at Viv and the scowl she had on her face told him if he touched her, he might have that black eye her brother had predicted earlier, so he kept his hands to himself.

The music from the jukebox changed to a soft melody, and a shadow was cast across him as Sarah stood beside him. "Can I steal you away for a dance?"

He had to give her credit. She was persistent. "Sorry, I'm just on my way out."

Finishing his beer, he stood up to leave and glanced at Viv. Her long, blonde hair was tucked inside a ball cap. He didn't know why she hid it because he imagined it would look lovely flowing over her shoulders. That led him to other thoughts. Her naked and on his expensive sheets, with her hair fanning out around her. Her naked and arm wrestling him at his dining room table. Her naked...

"Time for me to go."

Viv looked up at him. "Yeah, me too." She emptied her beer and put a twenty on the table. "I'll walk you out." She looked at Sarah. "Time to find another obsession."

Sarah smiled. "There's only one Red."

"Thank the stars for that," Viv said. "The world doesn't need that much trouble."

He wasn't accustomed to women fighting over him. Then again, Viv wasn't staking a claim. She was simply doing her job.

He wrapped his arm around her shoulder and led her toward the door. He would never forget that kiss nor the feeling it brought him—the taste of her lips still on his and the warmth of her touch yet in his heart. He smiled at the thought as they stepped out into the night.

At his truck, she opened his door and gestured for him to get inside. Everything seemed a bit backward—shouldn't it be the other way around, him opening her door?

"Get home and lock the door, and set the alarm," she said with an overdramatic flair, stretching out her arm as if she expected a tip. "Give me your phone."

He obeyed immediately, handing over his phone without question.

"This is my number. If there's any trouble with your stalker tonight, don't think twice about giving me a call."

She entered her number in his contacts and handed him back his phone.

"Do you think she'll come back?"

"Oh sure, she already did. Whatever you've got going on, she's at the front of the queue to buy it."

"I'm not selling anything."

Viv chuckled. "I know. I hear you give more free samples than a superstore launching a new meatball."

Red couldn't help but feel a pang of embarrassment at Viv's words. He had always been proud of his reputation as a ladies' man but hearing her speak casually about it exposed him. He wondered if Viv saw him as just a playboy and nothing more. Then he remembered the way she had looked at him earlier, the way she had kissed him so briefly but so fiercely. He couldn't deny that there was a connection between them, something that went beyond their professional relationship.

Red thanked her and slipped his phone back into his pocket. He climbed into his truck, feeling Viv's eyes on him as he started the engine. He didn't want to leave her, but he had to. As he pulled away, he saw her standing in the same spot, watching him go. He raised a hand in farewell, and she waved back.

Driving home, Red's thoughts drifted back to the kiss with Viv. It was a brief moment meant only to protect him from Sarah's advances, but he couldn't deny that he had enjoyed it.

When he arrived home, he locked up his house, but remembered that his security code was still visible on the website Anything for Love. He made a mental note to talk to Viv about changing it.

After a while, Red headed to bed. He was drifting off to sleep when he heard a creak on the entry floor. His eyes snapped open, and he immediately knew Sarah was in the house. He grabbed his phone, slipped into the walk-in closet, and called Viv.

"Viv, she's in the house," he whispered.

"Where are you?" she asked.

"I'm in my closet."

"Stay there. I'm on my way."

Red heard Sarah moving around in the living room. He retreated to the farthest corner, tucking himself behind his long winter coat, heart pounding, and waited for Viv to arrive.

"Red, baby, where are you?" Sarah's voice rang out. She was in the living room.

He'd had overzealous fans, but this was getting out of control. This was a scene out of *Fatal Attraction* minus the boiling bunnies.

"Red!" Sarah yelled. "I forgive you. Now come out."

She forgave him? What the hell was wrong with this woman? He'd done nothing wrong. As he tried to blend in with the drywall, he knew he'd done a lot wrong in his life. How many women had he used throughout his lifetime? Sure, they had used him too, but he should have been more chivalrous and discerning. He should have been more careful with their hearts and their feelings. But then you are what you learn. What else did he know?

Red's heart pounded as he crouched in the closet, waiting for Viv to arrive. He could hear Sarah moving around the living room, and he knew that he was running out of time. He tried to steady his breathing and focus his mind, but all he could think about was what would happen when she found him. Would she drag him to bed and have her way? That would have sounded grand in another lifetime, but he was tired of willing bodies writhing with animal drive when what he craved was connection and true affection. What he needed was a willing heart.

Suddenly, he heard the front door open, and a voice call out, "Honey, I'm home," and he knew Viv had arrived. Relief flooded through him, and he crept out of the closet, phone in hand. He could see Viv's silhouette in the dim light filtering through the curtained window and felt a sense of peace wash over him.

He watched Viv lead Sarah out of the house, her strong and confident stride filling him with admiration.

"If you come back, I'll have to shoot you," Viv said to Sarah.

He didn't know if she was serious, but she didn't sound like she was joking.

When she returned, he was in the kitchen making a pot of coffee. "What did she say?"

Viv sighed. "She said she'd be back and that there was enough of you to share."

He made them each a cup of coffee, and they sat at the kitchen table, sipping silently. He could tell Viv was lost in thought, her eyes dark and focused. He wondered what she was thinking about but didn't want to interrupt her.

Finally, she spoke. "You need to be careful, Red. Sarah is not someone to mess with. She's dangerous and unpredictable. Have you ever seen predators after their prey? They are singularly focused on their task, and Sarah believes you're the one. She told me she's already picked out your rings. She's delusional and possibly dangerous. These things can escalate very quickly. It's hard to know her real trigger."

Red eyes widened. He knew he couldn't just ignore the situation. He needed to be proactive, to take steps to protect himself.

"Did you say a hundred dollars an hour? No discount for twenty-four-hour service?"

Viv looked at him. "You want around-the-clock protection?"

He pointed toward the front door. "I think I need it, don't you? That's the second time she's come into my house."

"I'll talk to the sheriff tomorrow."

Red shook his head. "You can try, but he won't listen. He thinks I created this situation."

She smiled. "You did, and I can't blame him. Small towns have limited resources."

"What did you tell Sarah?"

Viv's cheeks turned radish red. "That I was your fiancée, and we were getting married."

Red was surprised to feel a warmth spread through him at those words. He'd been engaged once to the wrong woman. Cameron was amazing, but she was too good for him. Too nice. Too pliable. He needed someone who would keep him on his toes. He needed someone like Viv.

"You're hired, but you have to stay here. If you were truly my fiancée, you'd live in my house and sleep in my bed."

For a second, he thought she might reach over and slug him in the face, but instead, she leaned back.

"If I'm going to work this job, we need to get a few things straight. I'm not your fiancée, and I'm not sleeping in your bed. Also, to clarify, I'm in charge. If I say jump, you ask how high. If I tell you to do something, I want you to do it. Understood?"

He was usually the alpha in his relationships, but something about her confidence turned him on.

"Fine. You're in charge."

"So, here are the rules."

"I'm listening." He waited for her to outline a list a mile long.

"I have one rule."

"Only one?"

She chewed her lip and stared at him. "In your case, there are two. I make all the rules, and we are not sleeping together."

He nodded, but inside, he hoped she'd be breaking one of those rules, which wasn't the rule about rules.

"Can you start tonight? I don't want to have to confront this psycho on my own."

She finished her coffee and stood, taking the chair to the front door, where she wedged the back under the handle.

"I'm on the clock as of now. Since you were almost married to my sister-in-law, I'll give you the friends and family rate and only charge you eighteen hundred a day. By the way, I will need to bring in someone for a shift. I do need to eat and sleep sometimes too."

He laughed. "That's supposed to be a deal?"

"Take it or leave it."

"I'll take it, but Viv?" He walked up to her and leaned in, so his lips almost touched her ear. "I would have paid twenty-four."

CHAPTER NINE

Viv got as comfortable as she could on the couch, her mind racing between strangely personal thoughts of Red like his chiseled abs and his vulnerability, and the psycho stalker who would try to gain access to his house again. She knew she should be developing security system specs, safety protocols and protection scenarios, but the kiss she initiated to protect him still lingered in her mouth the way you still taste your favorite food even if you haven't had it in a while. She tried not to think about him that way; it was unprofessional and inappropriate, but she couldn't help herself. The damn man was twenty feet away, probably sleeping naked between soft sheets. For what he lacked in finesse and consideration, he sure made up for in igniting sheer desire. She had to blame the damn kiss that left her heart hammering long after his lips were gone. It's never good to have to improvise when you're protecting someone—was grabbing and kissing him the only play? Or maybe that voice in her ear reawakened a need in her.

His words seemed to echo in her mind as she drifted into a dreamlike state, a fantasy world of Red and her. They weren't romantic words. He said he would have paid what she originally asked, but that meant he valued her. She'd been looking for validation all her life, and here was a man willing to give her what she craved and deserved. When she thought about what she needed, she imagined them in a romantic embrace, their bodies intertwined, and her lips pressed against his. She let out a soft sigh as the desire in her heart surged. But as quickly as it had come, her fantasy vanished, leaving her cold and alone with only a throw pillow and an afghan to comfort her for the night.

SHE WAS JOLTED awake by a loud pounding on the door.

"If that's Sarah, I swear I'll kill her." Groaning, she stumbled to her feet and made her way to the door, still bleary-eyed from sleep. When she moved the chair and opened the door, she was shocked to see her brother Val standing there, a fierce scowl on his face.

"Val, what are you doing here?" she asked, confused.

Ignoring her question, Val marched past her and into the living room. "Where is he?"

Seconds later, Red appeared shirtless with pajama pants hanging low on his hips. "What's going on?" Val lunged at Red without a word, throwing a punch that caught him square in the jaw.

Viv tried to intervene, but Val pushed her aside and continued to pummel Red.

"What the hell is wrong with you?" Viv shouted, grabbing her brother's arm.

"You know damn well what's wrong!" Val yelled back, his face twisted with anger. "He seduced you."

Viv felt her face go red with embarrassment and fury. "No, he hasn't. Now stop this right now!"

Val stepped back, breathing heavily.

Red sat on the couch, rubbing his jaw, and looking stunned.

"What the hell is going on?" he asked, his voice shaky.

Viv took a deep breath, trying to calm herself down. She knew she needed to explain things to Val and Red, but she wasn't sure where to start.

"I... Red and I are working together. You know that," she said finally, her voice low. "He hired me to install a new security system in his house and provide personal protection advice."

Val looked at her. "And that required a sleepover?"

"His stalker came back. I'll be here from this point forward."

"Over my dead body," Val said.

"If Cameron didn't love you so much, and your daughter didn't need you as a father, I might consider that now. Geez, Val, I'm a grown-ass adult, and I get to decide who and where. And trust me,"—she pointed to Red—"it's not going to be with him and right here. I'm just doing my job. Nothing else."

Val looked at Red, then back at Viv, his expression softening slightly. "I'm sorry, Viv. I just... I don't want to see you get hurt, you know? And Red here ... he's—"

"I know he's an asshole, but so are you if you can't trust me to make good decisions for myself. Look, your wife saw something to love in Red and more to love in you. She's not an idiot and neither am I. I know what I'm doing."

"Fine. I trust you." He turned to Red. "But I don't trust you. If you try anything with my sister, I will return and finish the job." Val turned around and exited the house, leaving both Viv and Red alone. A red lump sat painfully on the chiseled edge of Red's jawline. "I'm sorry he hit you."

He rubbed the spot. "It's just karma paying me back for something I did. I probably deserve a lot worse."

"Let me get you some ice." She pointed to the couch where her blanket and pillow were. "Have a seat." Red opened his mouth to speak, but she shook her head. "Don't forget ... my rules."

He sank onto the couch and groaned while she hightailed it to the kitchen to get ice for his swelling jaw. When she came back, he was gone.

"Where are you?" she called from the living room.

"In bed."

He was going to push her at every turn. "I told you to stay put." She walked down the hallway and found his room at the end. She expected it to be a bachelor pad with a mattress on the floor and clothes strewn about, but what she found surprised her.

His bedroom was a far cry from what she had expected. The walls were painted in a soft, calming shade of blue, with a white accent wall behind the bed. The bed was a sturdy wooden frame with a plush white comforter and matching pillows. The room was immaculate, and everything was in its place. The dresser was dark wood, holding several carefully arranged picture frames and a four-wick candle. A subtle aroma of lavender filled the air, giving the room a soothing and tranquil feel. A nightstand held a lamp, a book, and a glass of water on one side of the bed. The curtains were drawn open, allowing the soft light of the rising sun to filter into the room, casting a glow over everything. She couldn't help but feel a sense of calm wash over her as she took in the peaceful surroundings.

"You were supposed to follow the rules."

Red was in bed with the sheet pulled halfway up his chest. "My head hurts."

"That's your ego." She pressed the ice to his jawline. "This is the injury."

"I don't want to cause you problems with your brother. I can try to find someone else to help me. Maybe I can beg Sheriff Cooper to reconsider."

He looked like a child, all tucked in and ready for sleep. She mindlessly ran her hands through his hair, brushing it aside so she could see his eyes. They weren't a simple blue, but a combination of blue and green, like the colors of the ocean meeting the shore. She hesitated momentarily, lost in their beauty, before finally mustering the courage to speak.

"Nonsense. You hired me, and I accepted the job. We are in this together."

"You sure?"

She smiled down at him and nodded. "I'm sure," she said, her voice gentle and reassuring. "Besides, I can handle my brother. And as for Sheriff Cooper, I think I have a better chance of convincing him than you do."

"True. Nobody seems to like me in this town, especially him."

"I like you." She snapped her mouth closed, but the words were already out. "I mean, you're okay for a—"

"Ass—" he started.

"Man," she finished. "I mean, we are dealing with the inferior sex."

He lifted his brow. "Now, that's your problem. You've been hanging out with the wrong men. Sex with me is never inferior."

"You're probably right, and that's why we have a Sarah problem. You sleep with them, and they turn into sex-crazed zombies."

"How long do you think she'll stick around?"

"Hopefully, she'll be a faint memory by next week. Why, are you afraid you can't afford me?"

Red let out a chuckle. "I can afford you just fine." He set the ice to the side. "I'm just wondering how many punches I'll have to take. I thought the idea was to keep me from harm. I mean, your brother threatened me within an inch of my life."

"Only if you tried anything. I imagine while you and Cameron may have found your own peace, Val might have some unfinished business with you."

He sat up and pulled her to him. "That kiss last night that meant nothing to you meant everything to me, and I'm happy to take another punch for a repeat. What do you say?"

There was a war waging inside of her. Sixty percent of her brain was leaning towards another kiss. In her mind, she justified all the reasons. The main one was that she had a personal policy to try everything legal twice because once wasn't always enough to decide. But the forty percent of her brain that was telling her to stop won because she knew getting involved with a client was bad news. Look at Val—he fell for Cameron, and now he was living in the boonies with a kid and a family of elk. Pulling at all her reserves, she kissed him on the forehead and jumped up. "I'm starving. Get dressed, and let's go someplace to eat." She nearly ran out the door. "Hurry before I get hangry."

She chastised herself for being so weak as she walked out of the room. All she wanted to do was turn around and kiss him again. There were lots of reasons to like Red. He was hot and talented and rich and a good kisser. He obviously was a great lover, or women wouldn't be breaking into his house to get into his bed, but bigger problems came with getting involved with Red. It was against her rules. He had once been engaged to Cameron. Her brother hated him. Those were the main obstacles, but there were others. He was a player, and she wasn't sure if he was interested in her or just wanted the thrill of reeling her in.

Twenty minutes later, he strode confidently toward her, his cologne enveloping her senses. It was a subtle yet alluring blend of cedarwood and pine, with just a hint of citrus.

Viv couldn't help but admire the way he looked, with his hair damp and tousled. Wearing faded blue jeans and a red flannel shirt, he had a rugged charm and effortless style that made her heart flutter. His shoulders were broad, and his chest was toned, with just the right amount of muscle definition.

He flashed her a smile as he sat on the couch across from her.

"So, you're hungry?" His voice was deep and alluring. It spoke to her on so many levels.

"Mmm hmmm." She stared at him, not thinking about actual food, but the kiss she turned down. "Starving," she said in a barely audible whisper.

"You have two options. You can have me or the diner."

Had she heard him right? "You?"

He laughed. "I can cook the pants off you, or we can go to the diner." There was a glint in his eye, and she was sure he had meant exactly what he initially said. If she opted for him, he would have tossed her over his shoulder like a caveman and taken her back to his bed.

"You cook?"

He stood. "I have lots of skills you don't know about."

"I'm afraid to ask." She rose and walked to the door. "I'll keep my pants on, thank you. Let's go to the diner." She knew if she stayed any longer, her forty percent hold on sanity would waver, and the weaker part of her would want to preview all his skills.

"You're afraid you might like it."

She marched out of the house and to her Yukon. She already knew she'd like it, but just because something was good didn't mean it was good for you. "Get in. I'm driving."

He locked up the house and went to his truck. "I'm driving."

She would have liked to battle him, but they were probably safer in his truck. While she could reach the gas and brake pedal if she sat at the edge of the seat, it didn't make for a comfortable ride. Besides, as a passenger, she could stare at him and find all his flaws, and by the time they got to the diner, she would be over this infatuation she had for him.

CHAPTER TEN

He felt her eyes on him as he drove away, her stare as precise and intense as a welding torch.

"Are you going to sit there and stare at me the whole time?"

She laughed. "It's like a two-minute drive. What's wrong? Can't handle the hot seat?"

"I can handle it. I'm just wondering what you're doing." He turned onto Rose and then took a right on Juniper.

"I'm looking for flaws."

He wondered if he should be offended or flattered. Did Viv think he had a lot, or was she at a loss to find one? Old Red would have laughed it off and told her he didn't have any, but he knew that wasn't true. He was like one of those big yarn balls—every string was a flaw. Somehow rolled up together, he made a semi-functional human being. He never wanted to unravel himself and see what was inside for fear that he would never be able to put himself back together again once he did. But maybe that was the beauty of life - the unraveling, the discovery, and the transformation that comes with it. Perhaps it was time to let go of his fears and embrace the possibility that the untangling might help him become a better version of himself.

"You'll need a longer ride than this." He turned onto Main Street and pulled into an empty parking space in front of the Corner Store. He immediately killed the engine and raced around the truck. Viv was the kind of woman who seemed to be self-sufficient, but he opened her door anyway. "I don't want to offend, but I like treating a lady like a lady."

She slid to the ground, looking at him like he'd grown a horn. "You realize you're giving me mixed signals, right? I mean, you're basically a manwhore, and yet you're acting like a gentleman."

He couldn't fault her for thinking so poorly about him. "They're not mutually exclusive. I am a gentleman—who has had a lot of sex with a lot of women."

"I'm sure all they talk about is your pillar of manners."

She walked to the diner door and waited for him to open it. When they stepped inside, the smell of bacon and syrup wrapped around them like a warm blanket. It was comforting, familiar—like coming home. He glanced over at her and saw a smile spread across her face. At that moment, he knew they were both thinking the same thing—pancakes.

As they took their seats, he couldn't help but feel grateful for her presence. He mostly ate alone in his kitchen, so this was special, and he wondered if they'd have anything other than Sarah to talk about.

Maisey strolled over with the coffeepot in her hand. "Hey, kids. What will it be today? Can I start you off with a cup of joe?"

With a puzzled look on her face, Viv asked, "Why do they call coffee Joe?"

Maisey set the pot on the table and touched her chin. "I

have no idea. Since it's a man's name, I imagine he had to be bold and bitter."

"Makes sense." Viv turned her mug over and watched Maisey fill it to the brim.

"You new in town?" Maisey asked, then turned to Red. "One of your fans?"

Red chuckled. "I doubt she's a fan. This is Viv. She's Val's sister."

Maisey poured him a cup of coffee. "You two a thing?"

"Nope," Viv answered far too quickly. "I'm his bodyguard."

"Another stalker?"

"He's had one before?" Viv asked.

Maisey laughed. "Girl, the line at his front door is longer than the bathroom line at the bar when it's girls' night out."

Viv's eyes popped open wide. "More than one a night?"

Red held up his hands. "Pleading the fifth."

"You two ready to order?" Maisey pulled out her pad and pen and looked at Viv.

"I'll have the hungry man's breakfast." She pointed to the item at the top of the menu.

Maisey wrote it down. "I like a girl who's not afraid to eat." She turned to Red. "What about you?"

He glanced over the menu. "I'll have pancakes and a side of bacon."

Viv stared. "I'm not sharing with you, so make sure you order enough. We've got a long day ahead of us."

He looked at the hungry man's breakfast. It had three eggs, hashbrowns, two pieces of sausage and bacon, and a whole stack of pancakes. "You're going to eat all of that?"

"Every single bite, and I might ask for more."

"I can't wait to see this."

Maisey put her pad away and picked up the coffee pot. "Me either."

Viv doctored her coffee with cream and sugar. "I'll arm wrestle you for breakfast."

"You want to humiliate me publicly? What did I do to you?"

She grinned, and his heart skipped a beat. "Shall I make a list?" She moved everything from the center of the table and rose to place her elbow there.

Red chuckled as he watched Viv position herself for the arm-wrestling match. He found her playful competitive spirit endearing, even though it resulted in finding himself on the losing end. He took a sip of his coffee, wiped his mouth, then raised his arm and locked his fingers with hers. "No cheating this time."

They both grunted and strained, their muscles bulging as they each tried to gain the upper hand. Red felt Viv's strength as she pushed against him, and for a moment, he thought she might beat him. But then he saw her smile falter slightly and knew he had her.

With a final surge, Red pushed Viv's arm onto the table, triumphantly declaring himself the winner. Viv groaned in mock defeat, but he could tell she was secretly pleased to let him win.

"You win."

He smiled. "That means you're buying breakfast."

"Happy to pick up the tab." She sipped her coffee and smiled.

This was way too easy. What was he missing? "Wait, you're expensing this to me, right?"

She laughed. "He's handsome and a genius."

"You think I'm handsome?"

She looked down at the table. "This job would be easier if you looked like a toad."

"I could be a toad if you promise to kiss me into a prince."

"I don't think there's that kind of magic in my kisses."

He reached across the table and took her hands. "Don't underestimate those kisses. I've had one, and it was magical."

She pulled her hands away. "I bet you say that to all the girls."

The truth was, he had some standard lines he used, but he'd never told a woman her kisses were magical. He might have been a womanizer in his day, but he was never a liar.

"Nope, you're my only magical kiss."

"What made it magical?"

He considered that for a moment.

He closed his eyes, trying to describe the inexplicable feeling that had surged through him when their lips had met. "It was like fireworks exploding in my heart," he said finally, his voice soft and reverent. "Your kiss was like a spell that transported me to another world where nothing else existed except you and me. I felt a connection that I'd never felt before, like we were meant to be together at that moment. That's what made it magical."

"Was it sparkler, ground, or aerial fireworks?"

He wanted to laugh, but the serious look on her face told him she was serious about the question.

"Definitely aerial. You know, the kind that soar high in the sky and explode into stars, comets, and shells?"

"What color?"

"Red, for sure."

"Hmmm, okay."

Now that he'd confessed, he wanted her thoughts on the kiss. "What did you think?"

She gave him a blank stare. "Of what?"

He let out an exasperated sigh. "Our first kiss."

"Oh. You mean our first and last kiss."

He shook his head. "It's only the last because it was the most recent, but I can assure you it won't be the final kiss. A kiss that sets off explosions inside me deserves an encore."

She waved him off. "I only kissed you so she couldn't."

"I know. But you could have left it at a kiss, but you added to it."

"I did not. It was a simple kiss. Nothing more."

"You cupped my face and leaned in. I thought you were going to climb into my lap." He shook his head. "You can lie to yourself, but I know what that kiss was."

"It was work." She frowned. "We call that improvisation. I had to put distance between you and the predator."

"How many kisses have you improvised in your line of work? I'm guessing mine was the first."

"I told you it was work."

"So, you get paid for kisses? And you said I was a ho," he chuckled.

Maisey showed up with her arms lined with plates. It looked like she was serving an entire family their meal, but all the plates were for them. "Who's a ho?"

"Excuse me?" Red asked.

"Who's callin' who a ho? This is a family establishment."

She placed the plates on the table with the lion's share in front of Viv.

"No one. We were talking about how—" he started.

"A simple kiss could be made into something it's not," Viv finished.

Maisey smiled. "Kisses never lie. They're either dynamite or duds. There's nothing in between. It's how I knew my Ben was the one." She pivoted and walked away.

"See. Kisses don't lie, and you shouldn't either."

"Fine, it was a good kiss, but I'm sure you could do better."

"Is that a challenge?"

She forked a bit of pancake and put it in her mouth. "So good."

He spent the next forty-five minutes watching her eat every single bit, just like she promised. She leaned back and patted her full tummy.

"Are you ready to go? We've got a lot of things to do today." She pulled out her phone. "First stop is the home electronics superstore in Copper Creek. We need more cameras and a new alarm pad with dynamic codes that you can change before someone else shows up at your door. Then we need to go to a hardware store to get a deadbolt."

"Do we need to get someone to install it?"

"I can do it."

"You're amazing."

She tossed out a couple of twenties and rose from the table.

"And apparently a professional kisser. Let's go."

CHAPTER ELEVEN

Viv sat in the passenger seat again. Usually, that would annoy her, but today, it fascinated her. She shifted her body ever so slightly. The angle made it possible to stare at Red without being obvious. He was a striking figure with a tall, lean physique that spoke of strength and athleticism. His chiseled jawline was accentuated by a hint of five o'clock shadow, giving him a rugged, masculine appeal. His mesmerizing eyes were framed by thick, dark lashes wasted on a man. But all of that, while appealing, was only a shell. What interested Viv more than anything was what he had on the inside.

"What did you want to be when you grew up?" she asked. It was always fascinating to find out what people's aspirations were when they were younger and see what they turned out to be. People rarely got the fantasy. In her case, how many Bavarian princes were looking for princesses these days?

"I wanted to be rich, so I didn't have to eat cheap frozen dinners for the rest of my life."

"Wow, didn't your mother cook?"

She watched his knuckles turn white as he gripped the steering wheel. "Maybe, but not for me. She left my father when I was an infant. She said it was because I was a boy, and I'd probably take after my father. She didn't want him, and she wanted no reminders of their life together."

A lump formed in her throat. She was exposed to a lot of people. Mostly teens and college-aged kids who were born to wealthy families. She'd never met anyone abandoned by their mother as an infant.

"So, you've never met her?"

"Nope, and I don't want to. Anyone who can walk away that easily isn't worth my time."

"What about your dad?"

He turned onto the highway that led to Copper Creek. The sign said it was a thirty-mile drive, so she had plenty of time to get to know Red.

"He did the best he could." He glanced at her. "What about you? What did you want to be?"

She laughed. "Taller."

"I suppose you should pick another goal."

"Well, I wanted to be a princess, but my hopes were dashed when Will married Kate."

"You and a million other girls."

"Sometimes you win, and sometimes you lose." She glanced outside at the scenery passing by. The storm had come and gone and didn't leave much snow. Only a dusting remained on the highest trees. She probably could have gotten away with the Mini Cooper after all. "Speaking of losing, what happened to you and Cameron?"

"I don't kiss and tell."

She respected that. "That's good to know because if my brother found out we kissed, he'd probably lose his mind."

Red reached up to touch his jaw. "He's got a good right hook."

"He's trained to win."

Red shook his head. "He sucker punched me. I had no warning."

"You didn't fight back."

He chuckled. "You should have figured this one out already. I'm a lover, not a fighter."

"My brother says you're a cheater. Which I'm sure he's thankful for, or he wouldn't have Cameron or Natalie."

"I'm an idiot." He quickly looked her way and then focused back on the road. "I'm a relationship saboteur."

She sat there for a few moments. Before she decided to become a bodyguard, she studied psychology, and she'd bet her next meal that being abandoned as a child made Red think he was unlovable. Who wouldn't believe that? If his mother didn't love him enough to stay, then what woman would want him?

She leaned against the door and stared out the window.

"Why do you think you do that?"

"Do what?"

"Sabotage your relationships." She stared ahead and saw a white ball of fluff on the side of the road. She was sure it was a towel or trash, but it seemed to be moving.

"I don't want to talk about it."

As they passed the fluff, she realized it wasn't trash but a tiny puppy. "Stop the car," she screamed.

He slammed on the brakes. "You're seriously going to get out of the car because I won't let you analyze me?"

As soon as he stopped, she hopped out and ran back fifty feet to where she'd seen the pup.

"Are you crazy?" he yelled out the open door. "You can't walk back to Aspen Cove. The highway is dangerous."

She ignored him, reached down, and swept the little thing up in her arms. "Oh my gosh, look at you." The puppy snuggled into her like she was its mom, and she wrapped her arms around it. "Someone abandoned," she lifted and looked between its legs, "him."

Red was standing between her holding the puppy, and the traffic whizzing by, like he was protecting them. "The mom probably hated the dad."

"Red, he's shaking."

He stopped flapping his arms like a spastic pterodactyl and walked with her to the truck. "What do we do with him?"

Red's face was pale, and his eyes were as big as saucers. "Take a breath, Red. You look like we just gave birth on the side of the road. It's a puppy, not triplets."

He helped her inside and gave the dog a gentle pet on the head. "I've never had a puppy."

Maybe Cameron was right. Maybe Red didn't know how to love, but that wasn't his fault. No one had taught him. A dog is a great place to start. *Where else do you get unconditional love, if you never got it from your mom*, Viv thought. "Meet your new dog."

Red stepped back, shaking his head. "No way. I can't have a dog."

"Why not?"

"Because..." He stared at her for a few seconds. "Because I don't know anything about dogs."

She cuddled the little guy to her chest. "He doesn't know much about humans, but he's giving us a chance."

Red stared at the puppy pressed against her chest. "I'd give you a chance if you tucked me next to your boobs."

"You mean my 58008s?" She still couldn't believe that was his password.

"You'll never let me live that down, will you?"

"Nope."

He rounded the truck and got inside. "Where to now?"

"We are on a mission. That hasn't changed. The only thing that has is there are three of us now." She looked down at the puppy, who had fallen asleep. "He'll need some supplies and a veterinarian appointment. We can also notify the animal shelter just in case he was lost and not left behind, although judging by his condition, he's been on his own a while." She pulled out her phone. "I'll make a list."

"Also billed to me, I'm sure."

She turned to him. "Well, he's not my dog. What are you going to name him?"

He stared ahead for a few minutes and then quickly glanced at the pup. "What about Lucky? I mean, he was lucky you saw him."

She smiled. "Lucky it is."

"We could name him Prince if you want."

His consideration touched her. "Not tall, dark, or handsome enough."

"You're setting the bar pretty high."

"Someone has to have some standards." She didn't mean to make it sound like he didn't, but in truth, he wasn't all that selective, but maybe while she was working for him, she could help him define a few things, like what ladies were worth his time. It was worth a thought. But right now, the number one question in her mind was, "Who named you Red?" She took a good look at his hair. It was more brown than anything else.

"My mother. The way my dad tells it, I came out screaming and was the color of a cherry. I guess I'm lucky they didn't name me Bing, Choke, or anything else that goes with cherry."

She pulled out her phone and looked up dogs and breeds to find out what kind of dogs came in white. "He's probably a mutt, but by the size of his paws, I don't think he'll get all that big." She kept scrolling through pictures and comparing them to Lucky. "I think he's either a terrier or a Bichon Frise."

"I suppose it doesn't matter. Nothing is going to change what he is."

"No, but knowing will help you determine his likely disposition. According to this article, if he's a terrier, he's likely to be stubborn and hard to train. People call them terrors."

"What about the other breed?"

"It says they are great family pets but need regular grooming and attention, or they can be destructive."

"What if he belongs to someone? I don't want to take a dog that already has an owner."

"If he has an owner, his owner isn't caring for him. The vet will check for a chip but let me say that this dog needs you. When was the last time someone truly needed you, and you stepped up?"

She watched as Red's jaw tightened and his lips pulled thin. After several agonizing seconds, he said, "Fine, I'll give him a month, but if he's not happy, or I'm not happy, we need a different plan."

They pulled into the electronics store, and she left Red with the puppy. "Lock the door."

"You think Sarah will show up here? She doesn't have a car. She told me she sold it to buy a ticket to the concert."

"Couldn't have been that nice a car."

"Hey," he said. "Our tickets sell for a premium."

"Either that's some expensive ticket, or she's got a shitty

car. I'm going with the latter." She exited the truck and shut the door.

It didn't take her long to find everything she needed, and when she got back, she knew Red would never get rid of that dog. He'd let him crawl under his shirt and snuggle against his bare skin. Lucky dog.

At the hardware store, she found a deadbolt and window locks that she could install that prevented the window from opening too far. On the way back to Aspen Cove, they stopped at a pet store and got Lucky a collar, a leash, food, and a kennel with a soft pad.

The day had turned out well considering how it started, but it all went downhill when they pulled into the driveway. The Yukon had been vandalized with red paint. The words "heart breaker" were sprayed across the side.

Before Red fully stopped, Viv was out of the truck and ran to the rental. "Oh, game on."

CHAPTER TWELVE

Viv told him to call the sheriff while she swept the house.

"This has gone too far." Red shifted Lucky to his other arm, pulled his phone from his pocket, and dialed the sheriff.

Aiden answered. "This better be life or death, Red. I warned you already."

"Sheriff, it's not about me. Someone has vandalized Vivian Armstrong's rental car. It's in my yard."

"I'll be right over."

"All clear," Viv said as she came back out and stood in front of the rental car. "This is going to cost a fortune to remove." She knelt and ran her hand over the red paint.

"I've got a guy." He called Bobby Williams, who answered right away. "Hey, Bobby, I've got a problem with some spray paint on a car. What do I do?"

Bobby wasn't one for long conversations. "Butter Wet Wax," was all he said.

"Got it." Red ordered it from Amazon, hoping to get a Prime delivery, and then he went to Viv. "I'll get this taken care of. It's my fault."

She stood and leaned against the SUV. "It's all part of the job."

"You've got a dangerous job."

"I'm not the one with the stalker."

"And she believes I'm going to marry her."

Sheriff Aiden Cooper pulled up, stepped out of his cruiser, and surveyed the scene as his boots crunched on the gravel of the narrow driveway. He took in the damage to the truck, cursive letters in blood red. He shook his head.

"Same one or another woman?"

"We think it's Sarah." Viv approached Aiden and held out her hand. "I'm Vivian Armstrong, head of Vortex Security."

Aiden's eyes widened momentarily, and Red knew precisely what he was thinking. How was this little bitty thing going to protect anyone? But Red had seen her in action, and she had more courage, not to mention smarts and reflexes, than most. She walked into his house knowing there was an intruder and didn't hesitate to act.

"Nice to meet you."

"Vortex, huh?"

She seemed to grow taller in front of him. It was apparent she felt a lot of pride in her position.

"Yes. Mr. Blakely has hired me to protect him from a fan."

The sheriff rubbed his jawline. "Would you still call her a fan after this?" He pointed to the SUV.

"I'd call her a problem, and we need your help. I don't have the authority to arrest someone, and I need to know that you'll come if there's a problem and we call."

"As long as lover boy over there isn't instigating problems, I'm happy to address real threats. Most of the time, I'm dragging women from his bed."

Viv looked at him and smiled. "I promise that Red will be as chaste as a virgin."

Aiden laughed. "Good luck with that." He moved toward the truck for a closer inspection. "Bobby should be able to help with this mess."

Red held up his phone. "I already talked to him. What he recommended is on order."

Lucky squirmed in his arms, but Red held him more tightly until he started to yelp.

"He wants down," Viv said.

Red placed the pup inside the white picket fence and watched as he sniffed and explored his new surroundings.

"Do you have security footage?"

Viv pulled her phone out, and several minutes later, they were watching the video of his yard, but the cameras only caught the front walk and the door. His existing system didn't cover the side of the house.

"It's got to be Sarah. She's the only one mad at me."

"This week," the sheriff said under his breath. "It's possible, but it could be someone else, too. Your system is inadequate."

Viv glared at him as if to say, "I told you so."

"We purchased additional equipment today. I'll get it installed in the next few hours. Next time she comes, we'll have her on camera. We will also be implementing new security protocols like not inviting people you don't know into your bed for starters—although this one did invite herself."

Lucky barked, and they all watched as he chased a bug around the yard.

"You got yourself a big bad watchdog, I see."

Viv laughed. "No, he's got himself a friend."

"We'll see how long that lasts. Red isn't known for his commitments."

He couldn't defend himself because the sheriff was right. The only thing he'd stuck to in his life was music.

"Now that's not fair, Sheriff," Viv said. "Sometimes, it takes some of us a long time to find our way. I think Red is on the right track."

"If you say so." The sheriff walked away, climbed into his patrol car, and drove off.

"You haven't made a lot of friends in this town. Why is that?"

"I can't help it if people don't love me."

"Maybe you can." She walked to the truck and got the bags of goods they'd purchased during their outings. "I find that for someone to love us, we often have to love ourselves first. I mean, think about it. How can you expect someone to love you if you can't stand yourself."

"I like myself."

"Okay, but when you look in the mirror each morning, do you love who you see?"

He hadn't given much thought to loving himself. He loved things about his life, like his ability to make music, but to look at himself and declare that he loved what he saw? No, he'd never considered that.

"Oh, I've loved myself plenty, and I'll tell you, it's not as satisfying as when I'm loving someone else."

She marched past him. "That's your problem. We wouldn't be here if you weren't spreading your love so far and wide."

She set the bags on the porch and started to unpack. "Do you have a ladder?"

"It's in the shed."

"Is it locked?"

"No, this is Aspen Cove. Nothing bad happens here."

She cocked her head and put her hands on her hips. "Except break-ins and vandalism."

Lucky growled and barked. When Red turned, he found the dog fighting with a flower, and by the looks of it, the flower was winning.

"You should feed him and see if you can get an appointment at the veterinary clinic in town. I'll get the cameras installed."

He'd just been dismissed. Sighing, he moved towards the door, holding the dog food in one arm, and sweeping the pup up with the other. He was now a dog owner—what had he gotten himself into? It's not that he wanted a dog, but he didn't want to disappoint Viv. With one last glance at Viv outside, tending to the cameras, he stepped inside his home.

The pup wriggled excitedly in his arms, then hopped onto the ground and sniffed around at everything with great enthusiasm: the rug, chairs, tables, and even his old guitar. His tail wagged fiercely as he ran around in circles, looking up now and again to see if his new "dad" approved of his behavior.

With a chuckle, Red dropped to his knees and patted his lap. "Come here, buddy. We have to go over some rules." The pup raced back over, jumping onto him, and licking his face all over. "No chewing on furniture. And you can only pee or poop outside. Got it? In exchange, I'll feed you and take care of you. But don't expect me to love you—that I can't do. How do ya like them apples?" Red sighed, stroking the pup's fur and trying to ignore Doc's voice in his head. He wasn't offering Lucky much—just a home, food, water, and a yard at best. He hadn't been emotionally capable of loving anything, or maybe he just hadn't given love an honest try. He imagined the safest place to start would be a pet.

After all, Lucky was just a pup; he deserved all the love he could get. Red had to admit that the little guy already had a piece of his heart, even if it was only a tiny sliver. He felt a kinship to the dog who'd been tossed aside and knew he had to do more than feed and care for Lucky if they had any chance of them forming a bond together. With that thought in mind, Red made an appointment with the local vet to get Lucky checked out and up to date on vaccinations. He also found a pet store online where he could buy toys and treats for Lucky—anything to help foster their growing relationship.

Red knew this puppy would change his life forever for better or worse—but deep down, something told him it would be for the better.

Feeling a newfound purpose, he set up the kennel and made Lucky comfy in front of the television. He scrolled through the channels, but the only thing that seemed to capture his interest was *Survivor*. Red thought it ironic since that's exactly what the dog was.

He moved into the kitchen and set out to make a meal that would blow Viv's mind. The woman had a hollow leg when it came to eating, and he would make sure she was satisfied. And maybe, in the process, he'd impress the pants off of her.

But as he chopped vegetables and seasoned the meat, Red couldn't help but wonder why Viv had such a hold on him. She wasn't his usual type; he typically went for taller and more conventionally feminine women. Yet, he found something about Viv's tomboyish demeanor and casual style alluring and disarming. Her smile made her approachable and almost inviting—although admittedly, inviting him she was not. Maybe it was how she held herself confidently and didn't seem to care about impressing anyone. Or perhaps it was her intelligence and quick wit that always kept him on his toes. Whatever it was, Red couldn't deny his attraction toward her, which scared him. Could she be the one? Or would she be another woman who left when things went south, and he knew they would. South was the only direction his relationships traveled. Girlfriends for a night were so much less complicated.

The door opened, and Viv walked in dripping sweat. "Can I borrow your shower and some clothes?" She looked down at herself. "Tomorrow, we have to go to Val's place to get my things."

"Can't we buy you new stuff? Do we have to visit your brother?" He rubbed his jaw. "I won't fully recover for a while and don't think I can sustain another blow."

"Don't be a baby. He's not going to hit you again. Besides, you have to stand up to bullies." She lifted her nose in the air. "Did you cook?" She moved to the trash can and looked inside. "What are we having?" She rummaged through the top of the garbage. "I don't see any boxes."

"I don't use boxes. I cook real food. We're having baked chicken and roasted vegetables with garlic mashed potatoes that I peeled, boiled, and mashed myself. As for bullies, I think I'll stay clear."

She stared at him. "Have you ever told Sarah you weren't interested in her?"

"I told her to leave my house. That should be pretty clear."

She scrunched her nose. "Yeah, you'd think, but not everyone hears the same message. Maybe when she comes back, the thing to do is to tell her you're not going to be her friend, fling, or fiancé."

"I told her you were my fiancée. That should be pretty clear."

"Maybe, but now she just sees me as an obstacle." She pointed to the kennel. "What's he watching?"

"*Survivor*. He's a fan."

"Aren't we all?"

"Dinner will be ready in fifteen minutes. Help yourself to whatever you need."

Red eagerly awaited her return, and when she did, he was awestruck. The oversized T-shirt hung off her shoulder, revealing a glimpse of her sun-kissed skin, while his boxers hugged her hips, showcasing her curves. Her wet hair flowed down her back in golden waves. He didn't think. He acted. He rushed over and pulled her into his arms, kissing her like she was the only thing that mattered in the world. The intensity of the moment took their breath away, and Red knew that this was something special. As she pulled away, he looked into her eyes and saw a reflection of his feelings staring back at him until she punched him in the jaw.

CHAPTER THIRTEEN

The soft morning light filtered through the curtains and woke Viv from her sleep. She was in a much better mood than she had been in days prior, feeling relaxed and refreshed. As she stepped out of her bedroom, the house was silent so she tip-toed down the stairs and into the kitchen. Red was still asleep, and Viv didn't have the heart to disturb him.

Her stomach grumbled which sent her searching through the cabinets and refrigerator like a treasure hunter seeking buried gold. The kitchen was as empty as a barren desert—no cereal, toaster pastries or convenience food in sight. Being the only girl in her family besides her mother, one would expect that she'd know how to cook but it had never interested her. The only thing about food she enjoyed was consuming it. People liked to tease her about her ravenous appetite, but they don't think about how much fuel it takes to maintain all that muscle, she mused, growing even hungrier.

She found some eggs, cheese, and a few slices of bread, and decided to make some simple scrambled eggs.

As she cracked the eggs into a bowl and started whisking them, she couldn't help but feel self-conscious. She had always been the underdog, and cooking was just another thing she felt inadequate about. Even her brother had cooked a dinner that would have made Martha Stewart proud.

Just as she was about to put the eggs in the pan, Red walked in holding Lucky. "Good morning," he said as he made his way to the coffee maker. "What's for breakfast?" He popped in a K-Cup and pushed start.

"I was just about to make some scrambled eggs," Viv replied, trying to sound confident. "I could use a cup of coffee."

"I got you." He waited for the first cup to finish brewing and handed it to her before he started the next. "Cream is in the refrigerator. Sugar is in the bowl." He pointed to a simple white dish on the counter. "What kind of eggs are we having?"

"Kind?" She looked in the bowl. "Chicken, I think? What did you buy?"

Red laughed and walked over to her, putting his hand on her shoulder. "Let me help you," he said, putting Lucky on the floor and taking the bowl of eggs from her hands. "I make a mean scrambled egg."

Viv watched as he expertly cooked the eggs, adding cheese and some herbs, and served them up on a plate with a few slices of toast. She leaned against the counter and took a bite. The eggs were fluffy and delicious, and Viv couldn't believe how good they tasted.

"Wow, these are amazing," she said, taking another bite. "How did you learn to cook like this?"

Red's smile faltered for a moment. "I had to learn how to cook to survive. I picked up a few things from my dad, but most of what I know, I taught myself or learned from cooking shows. The trick with eggs is to go slow, not too much heat all at once."

Viv felt a pang of sympathy for him. "You're a natural," she said, trying to lift his spirits. "Maybe you can teach me a thing or two."

He waggled his brows. "I'm happy to teach you everything I know in the kitchen and beyond."

She walked past him. "Your problem is you have a one-track mind."

Lucky barked frantically, desperation seeping through his eager eyes. She sighed and scolded him. "You're as bad as he is. You're both looking for the quick fix." She felt bad for bundling them together. Lucky was hungry. He couldn't help himself. Red on the other hand could, or could he? He was hungry for love, but indulged in sex like people eat junk food. It fills you up for a while but doesn't nourish your body or your heart, and it gets old really fast. "Let's finish eating and then head to my brother's. I can't live in your T-shirts and boxers forever."

"I'd argue that, but I know I'd lose," he muttered, forking his scrambled eggs with a vengeance.

"I'm glad. It's important to recognize one's limitations,"

"I suppose... but if you don't mind, I think I'll stay here." His voice wavered and he looked away from her.

She shook her head and crossed her arms. "Don't forget, when I took this job, you agreed to do what I said—and I say we're both going." No chance for negotiation here, no matter how much he pleaded silently with his eyes.

"What about the dog? He has a veterinary appointment in an hour."

Viv hadn't considered Lucky but didn't see why he

couldn't come too. "He's invited as well. We'll take him to the vet first, and then we'll head to the cabin."

"Fabulous," he said without enthusiasm. "How did you sleep?" he asked.

She tried to hide the smile tugging at the corners of her mouth. He suggested that they sleep together for safety, which was never going to happen, so she grudgingly accepted the spare room once she had the additional security cameras in place. "Like a baby, but I didn't wet the bed," she said before turning her head and looking away quickly. "How about you?"

He shook his head. "Having a puppy is like having a baby I imagine. He whined incessantly all night, and I eventually resorted to turning on the TV to settle him down. Unfortunately, there was no *Survivor* on, so he had to settle for *Alone*, but it had the wilderness and lots of animals and that seemed to do the trick. We didn't pee the bed either."

She hadn't thought about taking the dog outside to go potty or how dangerous that could be for Red. Her brother had told her she wasn't equipped for a job like this and maybe he was right. That was a big oversight. She'd have to be more diligent in the future if she were to keep Red safe.

Viv and Red finished breakfast, with Viv savoring every bite. After cleaning up, they each got ready, loaded Lucky into Red's pickup truck, and drove to Main Street. Aspen Cove had an undeniably picturesque charm. Viv admired the quaint storefronts in shades of pink, blue, and yellow that lined either side of the street, and she could see the bustling diner across from them that served up some of the best pancakes known to man.

As Red steered the truck into a parking spot in front of the vet's office, Viv craned her neck to read the tastefully simple sign. "Veterinary Clinic" was etched in white on a navy-blue background.

"They don't put much thought into naming things around here," she said.

Red killed the ignition and smiled at her, his eyes twinkling. "I don't know. There's a beauty to its simplicity." He leapt out of the driver's seat and moved quickly to open her door. As he gently took the pup in his arms, Viv slid off the seat and onto the pavement.

Red glanced up at the sign again before turning back to her with a smirk. "At least you know what you're getting."

They walked into the clinic and were welcomed by a cheery receptionist, who beckoned them to take a seat in the waiting room. Viv couldn't help but notice how nervous Lucky seemed. He whined and squirmed in Red's arms, as he yipped and wiggled like he was about to flee. Finally, the door to the exam room opened, and an energetic and effervescent young woman stepped out. "Hello, I'm Charlie," she said, extending her hand to Red.

Red shook her hand. "I'm Red, and this is Viv. We're here to get Lucky checked out."

Charlie nodded and led them into the exam room. She examined Lucky from the tip of his ears to the crooked bend in the end of his tail.

After the exam, Charlie sat down with Red and Viv to go over her findings. "Lucky is in good health," she said, smiling. "But I did notice that he doesn't have a microchip. It's important to get him microchipped, in case he ever gets lost."

"Is that something that comes with an app? You know, so if he gets out, I can just look it up and figure out where he's at?"

Charlie laughed. "No, the chip isn't a GPS system. It's

an identification system that gives Lucky the best chance of being returned to you should he get lost. But you can get a collar that has a place to put an Apple AirTag. That can help you keep track of him."

"Makes sense." Red nodded. "Thanks for letting us know. Do you know where the closest shelter is?"

"Shelter? Are you giving him up?"

Red shook his head so hard Viv thought he'd snap his neck. "Oh no, we found him, and we want to make sure nobody's looking for him."

Charlie thought for a moment. "I can have my receptionist Eden call the nearest shelters. Give me a few minutes."

She watched as Red drew Lucky in close to his chest. "Let's hope you're not taken."

"Looks like you're getting attached to the puppy," she said.

Red smiled. "Maybe a bit. He's a good dog. He peed on his pad last night." Red beamed like a proud father.

Viv couldn't help but feel envious of Red's easy affection for the puppy. She had never had a pet, and wondered what it would be like to have something of her own to care for and love unconditionally. She'd been practicing the motto "Self-care is self-love" for a long time; surely, she must be ready to love and care for something or someone else.

Charlie came back into the room a few minutes later. "Eden called the two closest shelters, but they haven't had any reports of a missing dog matching Lucky's description. Sadly, people abandon dogs for all kinds of reasons I could never understand. I'm guessing that's what happened to Lucky. I can chip him and make him yours, but that's like a marriage. The chip is the license."

The realization hit Red like a ton of bricks as Viv watched his golden complexion turn ghostly pale. He wasn't used to thinking about forever. He lived life in fleeting moments of pleasure quickly replaced by the next party or one-night stand. Saying yes to the chip was saying yes to Lucky forever, and forever was a scary word.

"Yeah," he said, "Let's do it. Someone tossed this little boy away and I won't be the next person to let him down."

Red got online and ordered an AirTag while Lucky got his microchip. After the procedure was done, Red scooped up the puppy and held him close.

"It's official," he said, his voice thick with emotion. "We belong to each other now."

Viv nodded and wondered if he realized he'd called the dog a little boy. "You're going to make him so happy." The trio headed to Viv's brother's cabin in the woods. "It's been a great day so far."

"It has. Do we really need to ruin it by going to your brother's place? My jaw can't take another Armstrong punch."

She reached over and pinched his cheek. "You thought that was a punch? That was a love tap."

"That was client abuse."

"You want to see abuse? Let me tell my brother that you tried to kiss me and see what happens."

He gasped. "You wouldn't."

She laughed. "No, I wouldn't because a dead client isn't a paying client. Besides, I like Lucky too much to orphan him."

"Thank you." Red pulled up in front of the house but turned his truck around, so it was facing the exit. "Just in case I need to make a quick getaway."

"Don't worry, I signed on to protect you and that means against everyone, including my brother."

He looked around. "We're in the woods. He could murder me and say it was a bear attack."

"He could, but he won't."

Viv led Red up the steps to the porch and knocked on the door. A few moments later, it opened to reveal Val.

"Viv," he said, his tone cordial but distant. "What brings you here?"

"I just need to get my clothes," Viv replied, trying to hide her disappointment at her brother's lack of enthusiasm.

Val stepped aside, gesturing for them to come in. "Everything is where you left it."

Viv made her way to the spare room, with Red following closely behind her. She opened her bag and began packing up her things. As she did, she couldn't help but notice the sound of the baby crying in the next room.

She turned to Red. "That's Natalie," she said, her voice filled with excitement. "Let's go see her."

Red looked hesitant, but Viv didn't wait for an answer. She made her way to the nursery, where Cameron was cradling the crying baby in her arms.

"Hi, Cam," Viv said, leaning in to kiss her sister-in-law on the cheek.

"Do you want to hold her?"

"Oh, I don't know. She seems unhappy."

Cameron smiled, holding out her arms. "She's been fussing all day. Maybe you can calm her down."

Viv hesitantly cradled the baby in her arms, rocking her gently. Natalie's cries turned into coos, and Viv felt a sense of joy spread through her. "Look at that. She likes me."

Cameron laughed. "Well, you are her favorite aunt."

Viv smiled. "I'm her only aunt."

"That doesn't mean you're not the best." Cameron looked past her to Red. "Hey, Red. What have you got there?"

"Just a dog we found on the side of the road."

"You rescued him?"

Red lowered his head, but Viv could see the tops of his ears turning pink. "Yeah. Took him to the vet and everything. It's like having a kid."

Cameron laughed. "You can say that when you start breastfeeding him."

"I'm out." Red spun around and walked out of the room.

After a few more minutes with Natalie, Viv relinquished her back to her mother's care and walked into the living room to find that Red had struck up a conversation with Val. To Viv's surprise, they seemed to be getting along well.

"You ready to go?"

"Yep." Red sprang up like a jack-in-the-box, his eagerness to leave evident in his every movement.

After saying their goodbyes, Viv and Red made their way down to the lake, with Lucky bounding happily ahead of them.

"You want to watch the sun set?" Viv asked.

"You asking me on a date?"

She shook her head. "If this were a date, which it is not, I'd expect wine and wooing and food, lots of food, starting with shrimp cocktail and ending with baked Alaska."

"Okay, noted."

They found a secluded spot on the shore and sat down. "Isn't it beautiful?" As the sun set behind the tall pines, the sky turned into a canvas of warm and vibrant hues. Shades of pink, orange, and yellow bled together, painting the sky with an ethereal beauty. The water reflected the colors, creating a stunning mirrored effect that seemed to stretch on forever. The ripples on the water's surface caught the last rays, turning them into golden ribbons that danced in the gentle breeze. The overall effect was one of tranquility and serenity, as if the world had paused for a moment to appreciate the natural beauty of the sunset.

For the first time in a long time, she felt like she was exactly where she was supposed to be. And as she looked over at Red, she had a sudden realization that he was somehow an important part of her journey.

CHAPTER FOURTEEN

Red awoke with the first light of dawn, the sun just beginning to peek over the horizon, casting a soft pink glow on the world. He couldn't help but think about the previous evening, watching the sunset with Viv by his side. There was something about the colors that danced across the sky, warm oranges, and purples, that stirred a longing deep within him, a feeling he couldn't quite put his finger on.

The memory of Viv's laughter, the way her eyes sparkled in the fading light as they watched a lone buck come to the water to drink, was etched into his mind. Her presence seemed to bring a sense of peace and comfort he hadn't experienced in a long time. But he knew he couldn't rush things; their connection was growing, but slowly, and he wanted to respect the boundaries she'd set. Besides, she'd probably deck him if he didn't.

The scent of pine trees and fresh mountain air filled his lungs as he stepped outside, the crisp morning breeze sending a shiver down his spine. The sounds of the awakening world surrounded him: birds chirping, and the rustle of leaves. It was a world so removed from the one he was used to, his world of packed concert halls and screaming fans, and he couldn't help but wonder if this was where he truly belonged. It was as if this was the first morning he'd ever awakened to the sounds of nature instead of the groans of the excesses of the night before. It was nice.

As he stood there brewing a cup of coffee and taking in the serene beauty of the morning through his kitchen window, an idea struck him. Viv's rental SUV was still vandalized and needed cleaning. He decided that he could surprise her by cleaning it off. He tiptoed back into his room to change, making sure not to wake Lucky. When he was in an old pair of jeans and a T-shirt, he gathered the Better Butter Wax left by Amazon on his front porch and got to work, scrubbing away the red paint and the harsh words that marred the black exterior. The effort required to remove the paint was almost cathartic, as if each swipe of the cloth was also erasing some of his mistakes, little by little.

However, he had barely finished when he heard the front door open and close, followed by quick footsteps approaching. He looked up to find Viv with Lucky in her arms, her eyes wide and her face a mixture of anger and concern.

"What the hell are you doing?" she demanded, her voice sharp as she took in the scene before her.

"I wanted to surprise you," Red explained, trying to keep his tone light, but her expression remained hard. "I thought it would be a nice thing to do."

"Nice?" Viv's voice rose, as she set Lucky down. "Red, you're taking unnecessary risks by leaving the house without me. That's the whole point of me being here, to protect and keep you safe! How can I do that if you keep wandering off on your own?"

He could see the worry in her eyes, and he realized that she was right. He had been careless, so focused on doing something for her that he hadn't considered the potential consequences.

"I'm sorry," Red said sincerely, dropping the cleaning cloth and taking a step towards her. "I didn't think about it like that. I just wanted to do something nice for you, to show you how much I appreciate what you're doing for me."

Viv's expression softened, but her arms remained crossed. "I appreciate the gesture, Red, I really do, but I am not the priority here, you are. I can't protect you if you're not on board. You're paying me to be here. Let me do my job."

Red nodded, understanding the weight of her words. "I'll be more careful. I understand. I won't let my guard down again and I won't forget my place."

"Good," she said, her voice still firm but gentle. "Now, let's get inside and get cleaned up. We've got more work to do."

As they walked back into the house, Red couldn't help but feel grateful for Viv's presence in his life. She was a force to be reckoned with, strong and determined, but also kind and compassionate. He realized that he not only needed her for protection but also as a friend and confidante. He could trust her, and more importantly, he could be himself, not the person everyone else expected him to be. The truth is he was feeling lonely, unfulfilled, and unsafe before Viv entered his life. She made him feel better, whether it was her job or not.

The day unfolded with a renewed sense of purpose. Together, they installed a few more sensors and cameras to cover every possible entry point. He had to give Viv credit. She was thorough. As they worked side by side, they exchanged easy banter and teasing, both finding comfort in the other's company. After a while, Red decided to challenge Viv to a contest.

"Alright, Viv," he said, grinning mischievously. "Let's see who can tell the first two jokes to make the other person laugh. Winner gets bragging rights."

Viv raised an eyebrow, accepting the challenge. "You're on, Red. Prepare to lose."

Red went first, trying his best to come up with a joke on the spot. "Why don't scientists trust atoms?"

Viv pursed her lips, trying to keep a straight face. "I don't know. Why?"

"Because they make up everything!" Red delivered the punchline with a flourish, but Viv managed to suppress her laughter, offering him a polite smile instead.

"Nice try, but not quite there. My turn," she said. "Why did the scarecrow win an award?"

Red scratched his chin, genuinely curious. "I don't know. Why?"

"Because he was outstanding in his field!" Viv said triumphantly. Red couldn't help but chuckle at the corny joke.

"One point to you, Viv," Red conceded, before launching into his second joke. "Okay, why did the bicycle fall over?"

Viv shook her head, not knowing the answer. "Why?"

"Because it was two-tired!" Red waited for her reaction, but once again, Viv managed to keep her laughter in check, smirking instead.

"Alright, my turn again," Viv said, feeling confident. "Why couldn't the bicycle stand up by itself?"

Red furrowed his brow, puzzled. "I don't know, why?"

Viv grinned, delivering the punchline. "It was two-tired!" With a grin, she went "Ba-dum-tss!" as she slapped her thigh, adding a comical flair to the moment.

Red burst into laughter, partly because of the joke, partly because of her antics, but mostly because he couldn't believe she had used his punchline. "Not fair, you stole my joke!" he exclaimed, but he couldn't help smiling.

Viv laughed along with him, basking in her victory. "I guess great minds think alike. Better luck next time."

Their laughter filled the room as they continued to share jokes and stories, the friendly competition bringing them closer together. As they worked, Viv took the opportunity to discuss a safety plan with Red. They paused their work, sitting down on the living room floor amidst the tools and equipment.

"Red, it's important that we have a plan in case there's ever a threat," Viv said seriously, her demeanor shifting from playful to focused. "I need you to understand exactly what to do and where to go if something unexpected happens."

Red nodded, his own expression sobering as he realized the gravity of the situation. "Alright, what do you want me to do?"

Viv led him through the house, pointing out various hiding spots and escape routes. She showed him a tiny closet underneath the stairs that she'd equipped with a secure lock.

"If there's ever a serious threat, I want you to hide in here," she instructed. "It's not ideal, but it's the most secure place in the house. When you're inside, wait for my signal or the authorities to arrive before you exit. We also need a code word, something that will alert you to go into hiding without raising any suspicion."

"How about 'pineapple?'" Red suggested with a half-smile, trying to lighten the mood.

Viv chuckled. "Alright, 'pineapple' it is. But remember, this is serious. If you hear that word, you need to act immediately."

Red nodded, the weight of her words sinking in. "I understand. I'll be ready. Do you really think someone will try to hurt me?" He could tell by the look on Viv's face, the answer was yes. He couldn't help but be impressed as she talked about ongoing security assessments, surveillance, threat mitigation, routines, and other safety protocols, along with the countless security system enhancements—all to keep him from harm.

With their safety plan established, they continued working, their bond growing stronger as they shared in the labor.

That evening, after they had finished their work, they sat on the porch together, sharing a meal and talking about everything and nothing. The conversation flowed effortlessly, and Red felt a warmth in his chest that had nothing to do with the setting sun. As the sun fell behind the mountain, Red couldn't help but steal glances at Viv. He wondered if she felt the same way he did, if she also sensed the electricity that seemed to crackle between them. He wanted to reach out, to brush a strand of hair from her face or to feel the warmth of her hand in his, but he held back, unwilling to jeopardize the bond they were forming.

The sky darkened and the first stars appeared. Red dared to hope that their relationship was slowly, but surely, moving in the right direction. He knew that they had to take their time, to let the slow burn of their desire kindle and grow, but he couldn't help but feel excited about what the future might hold.

As they sat there, side by side, Red couldn't shake the feeling that Viv was more than just a bodyguard or a friend. She was becoming an integral part of his life. Someone he could trust and rely on. He'd never really had that type of relationship with anyone. She knew he was vulnerable and expected that of him. He'd never allowed that to happen in any relationship and there was something freeing and healing about having her in charge, at least for now. He'd never felt safer.

In the growing darkness, Lucky jumped onto the porch, a stray pinecone clutched in his jaws. With a playful woof, he dropped the pinecone at Red's feet, his tail wagging enthusiastically.

"Well, look at that," Red said, amusement in his voice. "I think someone wants to play."

Red chuckled, as he reached down to grab the pinecone and tossed it for Lucky, who bounded after it with unbridled joy. The simple act of playing fetch with the dog created a heartwarming scene, and he couldn't help but notice Viv's smile as she watched them.

Later that evening, after they had finished the last of their work for the day, Red decided to prepare a delicious dessert for both of them as a token of appreciation. He made a decadent chocolate lava cake, the enticing aroma wafting through the house. Viv couldn't help but marvel at Red's culinary skills as they sat down to enjoy it.

"This is amazing," she said, taking a bite. "I didn't know you could cook like this!"

Red grinned, pleased with her reaction. "It's a hidden talent. I find cooking to be therapeutic, and it's a nice way to unwind after a long day. Besides, a lot of women find it very sexy. Oh heck, why did I say that? I know I'm just another target in need of protection to you." He laughed as she saw Viv's lips turn upward into her beautiful smile.

As they enjoyed their dessert, Red suggested they watch a movie together. They settled on *The Breakfast Club*, a classic film they both loved. They curled up on the couch, the flickering screen casting a soft glow over the room.

As the movie played, Red couldn't help but provide his own commentary, offering insights into the characters and sharing his favorite quotes.

Viv glanced at her phone, drawing her attention away from the screen. She turned to Red, her voice steady.

"Pineapple, Red. Now."

Without hesitation, Red sprang into action, his heart pounding as he remembered their safety plan. He darted to the closet under the stairs, slipping inside and locking the door behind him. He hoped that whatever threat they faced could be resolved without harm to either of them. He knew that Viv would do everything in her power to keep him safe. The role reversal struck him as odd—every instinct in him wanted to stay and protect her, but disrespecting her rules would be disrespecting her and everything she worked for. He couldn't do that. He believed in her.

CHAPTER FIFTEEN

After Viv microwaved popcorn, she settled back onto the couch, a smirk playing at the corners of her mouth as she reveled in her prank. There was no threat, unless it was her taping his mouth closed. The code word had been perfect for getting Red to stop talking during the best part of the movie, but she hadn't expected him to react so quickly, disappearing into the closet without a second thought. That he had taken her safety plan so seriously was amusing and endearing.

In the dimly lit room, the flickering light from the television screen cast shadows on the walls, painting them in a soft green hue. The scent of the chocolate lava cake still lingered in the air, a warm and inviting aroma that reminded her of the closeness they had shared earlier. The sound of the movie's dialogue filled the room, punctuated by the occasional laughter of the characters on screen.

As she watched the movie, she couldn't help but steal glances at the closet door, curious how long it would take Red to realize it was a false alarm. Her heart pounded in her chest with anticipation, and she held her breath as she waited for him to emerge.

Finally, fifteen minutes later, the closet door creaked open, and Red stepped out into the living room, his eyes wide with confusion and surprise. He looked around the room, taking in the peaceful scene before him, and then turned his gaze to Viv, his expression a mixture of disbelief and amusement.

"Viv," he said, his voice filled with mock indignation, "did you seriously use our code word just to get me to stop talking during the movie?"

Viv couldn't help but laugh at his reaction, her eyes twinkling with mischief. "Guilty as charged," she admitted, a grin spreading across her face. "I had to do something to get you quiet during the best part. And I had to test our plan. I'm happy to say it worked."

Red shook his head, chuckling as he walked back to the couch and sat beside her. "You got me good," he said, reaching for a handful of popcorn from the bowl on the coffee table. "But I'll get you back."

Viv raised an eyebrow. "Oh? And how do you plan on doing that?"

"If I told you, you'd be anticipating it." Red winked at her, a mischievous glint in his eye. "It'll come when you least expect it."

As they resumed watching the movie, Viv couldn't help but notice the warmth that radiated from Red's body as he sat beside her, the heat seeming to fill the space between them. She found herself drawn to him, her senses heightened by his presence. The sound of his laughter, the feel of his arm brushing against hers as they reached for the popcorn, the sight of how his eyes crinkled when he smiled

—all of it made her heart race in a way that she hadn't experienced in a long time.

The movie continued to play, but Viv struggled to focus on the screen, her thoughts consumed by the man beside her. She knew it was dangerous to let herself feel this way, that her job was to protect him, not fall for him. But as the night wore on, she couldn't help but wonder if it was already too late.

Viv was startled by the sound of a soft thud from the room's corner as the final credits rolled. Turning her head, she spotted Lucky stretched out on the floor, his tail wagging gently.

Red noticed her attention shift to the dog and followed her gaze. "He probably needs to go out," he said. "The night air might do us all some good."

Viv hesitated momentarily, wondering if it was wise to spend more time together. But the thought of the crisp night air and the opportunity for more conversation was too tempting to resist. "Sure," she agreed, her heart swelling with anticipation.

They slipped on their jackets and clipped Lucky's leash to his collar. The dog practically vibrated with excitement at the prospect of a late-night adventure. Viv took a deep breath as they stepped outside, reveling in how the cool air filled her lungs and sent a shiver down her spine. Or was the shiver caused by Red?

The street was bathed in the soft glow of the moonlight, casting a peaceful, almost magical atmosphere over the road and houses. The night was quiet. The only sounds were the soft patter of Lucky's paws on the pavement and the gentle rustle of the leaves in the trees overhead.

As they strolled down the sidewalk, Viv and Red began reminiscing about their favorite parts of the movie. Their voices were hushed as if they were sharing secrets in the stillness of the night.

"I loved how many misfits came together in the end," Viv admitted.

Red chuckled, his breath visible in the cool air. "I love how the bad boy got the girl."

"Only until detention was over."

"You don't think they stayed together?" he asked.

"Oh, come on, this is the real world. Bad boys win for the moment because they are bad, and women want to live on the wild side, but only for a moment. In the end, they want the white picket fence."

He laughed. "Look at that. I've got both. I can give it all to you. I'm the bad boy with the white picket fence."

The warmth of their laughter seemed to chase away the chill in the air, and Viv found herself drawn even closer to Red. She could again feel the heat radiating from his body as they walked side by side, and she couldn't help but take note of the way his eyes sparkled in the moonlight.

As they continued to discuss the movie, Viv became more engrossed in their conversation. It was as if they had tapped into a wellspring of shared interests, each new topic leading to another, each moment deepening their connection.

They delved into the finer details of the film's plot, dissecting the characters' motivations, and speculating about possible alternative endings. It was a rare treat for Viv to find someone who shared her passion for old iconic movies.

At one point, their conversation turned to the movie's soundtrack, and Red began to hum one of the catchier tunes. Viv joined in, and soon they were laughing together as she butchered the melody.

Lucky trotted happily ahead of them, occasionally stopping to sniff at interesting scents or chase after a rustling leaf. The sight of him so carefree and content warmed Viv's heart, and she found herself grateful for both the dog and the man walking beside her.

As the night wore on and they looped back towards Red's house, a pang of sadness at the thought of their evening ending stabbed at her heart. Viv had always been a city girl, born and raised. Even though she'd spent most of her life on Centre Island, the bustling streets of New York were only a train ride away. The noise, the crowds, and the never-ending energy had been her life for as long as she could remember. But as she walked alongside Red that evening, she couldn't help but appreciate the tranquility and simplicity of small-town life under a starry sky.

Viv noticed that Red seemed more relaxed than she had ever seen him. His usual air of bravado had been replaced with a genuine vulnerability that she found both surprising and endearing. They spoke candidly, their conversation flowing naturally as they delved into the stories and experiences that had shaped them into who they were today.

"I never thought I'd say this," Viv confessed, "but there's something undeniably charming about this place at night. I mean, New York has its beauty, but it's nothing like the peace and quiet of a small town."

Red smiled softly, his eyes crinkling at the corners. "You know, I felt the same way until you came along. I thought small-town life wasn't for me but seeing it through your eyes has made me appreciate its magic."

As they continued to stroll, they opened up to each other about their personal lives, sharing stories and revealing vulnerabilities and insecurities. Viv spoke of growing up the youngest child and the only girl in a family of six brothers. Her family had run a bodyguarding business ever since she could remember, and she had always felt the weight of expectation on her shoulders.

"I am constantly trying to prove myself, you know?" Viv said, her voice tinged with both sadness and determination. "It's like I'm living in the shadow of my brothers, who are naturally gifted at the family business. But I never let that stop me. I work hard and do everything I can to make my mark, to show that I am just as capable as they are."

Red listened intently, his gaze never leaving her face. "That's incredible, Viv. You're a fighter. And you've clearly made a name for yourself. You should be proud of everything you've accomplished."

She blushed at his words, touched by the sincerity in his voice. "Thank you. That means a lot."

As they ventured further down the path, they stumbled upon a scenic spot where the wildflowers seemed to dance in the moonlight, the silvery beams painting a breathtaking canvas. A nearby stream gurgled softly, its crystal-clear water reflecting the shimmering stars above. They paused to take in the view, sharing a quiet, intimate moment as they stood side by side.

"You know, Viv, people have always misunderstood me," he admitted, his voice low and vulnerable. "I've been labeled a womanizer, but the truth is, I've just been trying to fill a void in my life. I've been searching for something real, something meaningful, but I've never found it."

Viv looked at him, her heart aching with empathy. "It's because you're looking in the wrong places. You can't find forever in a one-night stand."

Red nodded. "That's true, but relationships are scary."

"Anything new is scary, but you have to try at least.

You'll never find your forever if you're always looking for your right now."

He kicked a stone from the ground, rolling it into the stream. Lucky chased after it until he met the end of his leash, keeping him safe and dry. "You're right, there's more to life than empty connections."

Warmth spread through Viv's chest, her heart swelling with affection for this man who had allowed her to see a side of him that few others had. She reached out, placing her hand gently on his arm, offering comfort and understanding.

"I believe that we all have the power to change our lives, to fill those voids with something meaningful," she said softly. "Sometimes, all it takes is faith in ourselves and the willingness to open our hearts." She added that last bit for Cameron because she'd said that she didn't think Red knew how to love, but to love, one needed to let their heart lead.

Red turned toward her, his expression filled with hope and gratitude. "I'm grateful that our paths crossed, and I've had the chance to get to know you. You see me. I mean, truly see me. Not the musician or the money. You see the man. You make me want to be better."

"And you make me feel bad for using the safety word."

"You should feel bad. That was a dirty trick."

"It was, and I'll make it up to you."

"Oh yeah? How?"

"I'll make you breakfast tomorrow."

"You don't cook."

"I don't, but I can toast a Pop-Tart, which I picked up at the store."

"They had toaster pastries at the hardware store?"

She shook her head. "No, silly, they were at the electronics store, right by the register. They know their clientele. Computer geeks are rarely as skilled in the kitchen as Bobby Flay. We need quick and easy."

He smiled. "I know all about quick and easy."

She rolled her eyes. "We're talking about food and not women."

"Pop-Tarts it is. Please tell me that you got strawberry."

"How about I surprise you."

He laughed. "I'll be surprised if you can toast it without burning it."

"That's a fair concern." At that moment, she realized that she had found something in Red—a connection that went beyond the superficial, a bond that transcended the barriers of their pasts and allowed them to see each other for who they truly were.

She took his hand and intertwined their fingers, and they continued their walk back to the house. Lucky trotted alongside them, his happy panting punctuating the comfortable silence between them. As they approached the front door, Red asked, "What are you going to do now?"

"I'm going to bed. What about you?"

They entered, and he let Lucky loose from his leash and hung it by the door. Then he stood there staring into her eyes. "I'm going to kiss you if you promise not to punch me."

She stepped back. "Do you think that's wise?"

He shook his head. "No, but it's necessary."

Before she could put any more distance between them, he took hold of her shoulders and pulled her close. She was in his arms, and his lips were on hers, sending sparks of electricity through her body. The feeling was so intense that she felt as though she might faint, and for a few moments, she let herself be enveloped in the warmth and pleasure of his embrace.

He looked into her eyes and smiled, an expression that seemed to come from somewhere distant. "Good things should never be rushed," he said, sliding his hands down her arms, leaving a trail of warmth in their wake. He kissed her forehead and the tip of her nose, then stepped back and glanced at her hands as if he'd find them fisted and ready to strike, but she didn't want to hit him. She wanted to fall into his arms and stay there forever.

She felt a sudden chill at his departure, though her heart still beat wildly. She wanted to ask him to stay, to hold her again and never leave, but the words didn't come. Instead, she stared at him and hoped he'd see it in her eyes.

He pulled her close to him, and suddenly his lips were open, and his tongue was on hers. She felt the heat of his embrace and tasted the sweetness of his kiss all the way to her toes.

Step away, the voice in her head said, but she ignored it and stepped into the kiss, wrapping her arms around his neck, and pressing her hips to his.

His hands moved around her back as the kiss deepened. A moan breached the silence. *Was that her?*

He pulled away, putting distance between them. "I'm sorry," he said.

"No, don't be." She stood there for a second, catching her breath.

He took her hands in his and looked at her. "I should go."

She wanted to tell him he should stay and continue kissing her, but she knew that to do so would put them in a position that one of them would regret. Instead, she nodded.

"This isn't over, Viv. It's just beginning. The problem is I don't know how to start at the beginning. I usually jump in just before the end." He kissed her one more time. This time it was gentle and sweet. He moved back and smiled. "I'll need your help with that." He turned and walked away, leaving her standing alone, wanting so much more.

CHAPTER SIXTEEN

Red awoke with a start, his mind still reeling from the passionate kiss he had shared with Viv. As he lay there, his heart pounding, he couldn't help but feel a mix of excitement and apprehension.

As Red swung his legs over the edge of the bed and stretched, the morning sun's warmth filled the room. Making his way to the bathroom, he couldn't help but think about Viv. After a revitalizing shower, Red stood before his closet, mulling over his clothing choices. He wanted to look nice for Viv, to show her that he valued her presence and appreciated her as a colleague and a person.

Feeling silly for worrying about his clothes, Red searched his closet for the perfect balance between casual and polished. He briefly considered wearing his lucky socks with pineapples on them but quickly dismissed the thought. He chuckled at the idea of Viv's reaction, but that wasn't quite the impression he was going for. Besides, she'd no doubt say the word pineapple, which would send him scurrying into the cupboard under the stairs. *When had he turned into Harry Potter?*

Ultimately, Red chose a comfortable pair of well-fitting jeans and a flattering Henley shirt. He looked at himself in the mirror, content with his appearance, but couldn't help laughing at the notion of him fretting over his outfit like a teenager going on a first date.

Red found Viv in the kitchen preparing breakfast, her silky hair tumbling over her shoulders as she moved gracefully around the room. He couldn't help but steal glances at her, his mind consumed by the memory of their electrifying kisses.

As he entered, Viv flashed a sheepish smile and confessed, "I hope you're not expecting a gourmet breakfast because all I can manage are Pop-Tarts."

Red chuckled. "Well, you did promise Pop-Tarts, so I guess I can't complain."

Viv's face lit up with mock indignation. "Hey, at least I'm staying true to my word!"

She pulled a box of cinnamon sugar Pop-Tarts from the cupboard, causing Red's face to fall slightly. He had been secretly hoping for his favorite, strawberry.

"Ah, cinnamon sugar," Red teased, trying to hide his disappointment. "I was hoping for strawberry, you know. At least there would have been some semblance of fruit."

Viv laughed and playfully nudged him. "Oh, don't pretend you're a health nut. I'd never believe that after the lava cake. Besides, you're getting a delicious breakfast pastry. How bad can it be?"

Red grinned and decided not to press the issue further. He admired her for admitting her culinary shortcomings and appreciated her effort to provide breakfast.

As they waited for the Pop-Tarts to toast, Red couldn't help but tease Viv more. "Well, I guess I'll just have to cherish these cinnamon sugar Pop-Tarts, knowing they were made with love."

Viv rolled her eyes, but her smile betrayed her amusement. "Don't push your luck, mister."

They shared a quiet breakfast. Their conversation was stilted and cautious, as though they were tiptoeing around the unspoken emotions that hung heavy between them. Viv, eager to break the silence, suddenly piped up. "I put cream in your coffee; that's dairy, and a food group, you know."

Red raised an eyebrow, feigning surprise. "Wow, Viv, really going all out with the balanced meal here. Pop-Tarts, coffee with cream... What's next? A side of spinach?"

She smirked. "Oh, don't tempt me. I might serve you a kale smoothie for lunch."

Red shuddered playfully. "You wouldn't dare."

Viv leaned in closer, her eyes twinkling with mischief. "Try me."

"Probably a baseless threat, given your lack of kitchen skills. Do you even know how to make a smoothie?"

"Fine, you got me."

The lighthearted banter helped ease the tension, allowing them to enjoy breakfast. As they laughed and teased each other, it was almost as if the weight of their unspoken feelings had temporarily lifted, and they could be nothing more than two friends sharing a meal.

Red took a sip of his coffee, savoring the rich taste of the cream. He always drank his black. "I must admit, the cream does make a difference. I might just have to make it a regular thing."

Viv grinned, pleased with herself. "See? I told you. I may not be a culinary genius, but I know something about coffee."

They continued to chat and laugh, enjoying the fleeting

moments of normalcy amidst the whirlwind of emotions they were both experiencing. And even though they knew they couldn't avoid their feelings forever, for now, they were content simply to enjoy each other's company.

Red wondered how they could navigate their growing feelings while respecting their professional relationship. Their situation was unusual, and he knew they would have to tread carefully if they wanted to protect their hearts and careers.

As they finished their breakfast and cleared away the dishes, Red couldn't shake the nagging feeling that something needed to be said. The silence between them was becoming unbearable, and he knew they couldn't continue ignoring the elephant in the room.

"Viv," he began, his voice cracking with the weight of his emotions. "About last night..."

Viv looked up at him, her eyes filled with longing and apprehension. "Yes?"

Red took a deep breath, gathering his courage. "I don't regret what happened. In fact, I can't remember the last time I felt so ... connected to someone. But I know our professional relationship complicates things."

Viv sighed, her eyes filled with a mixture of vulnerability and determination. "You know, my feelings for you are making me break all my rules. I have a rule that says never get involved with a client." She paused momentarily, then continued, "I've never been in a situation like this before, and I don't want to jeopardize my reputation or our safety. But I can't deny that I feel something for you, something that goes beyond the boundaries of our relationship with you as my client. You hired me to protect you. That's really my priority and I don't want to do anything that would jeopardize that."

Red sighed in relief, grateful that Viv was willing to address their feelings head-on. "So, what do we do? How can we explore this connection without compromising our work?"

Viv bit her lip, clearly deep in thought. "Maybe we can set some boundaries. We can agree to keep our personal feelings separate from my professional duties for now."

Red felt a surge of hope as he considered Viv's proposal. It was a sensible approach that would allow them to cautiously explore their feelings while still maintaining the integrity of their professional relationship. "I think that's a great idea," he agreed. "Let's promise to be honest with each other and communicate openly about our feelings and any concerns we might have."

However, as the reality of their situation sank in, his hope began to wane. The truth was that they were constantly working together, and it seemed impossible to separate their personal and professional lives. They never had time outside her work to be just the two of them, and he couldn't help but feel disappointed.

"Viv," Red said hesitantly, "I'm not sure we can separate things like that. We're always together, and there's never really a moment when we're not involved in our professional roles. How do we navigate this without blurring the lines too much?"

Viv's expression mirrored his concern, and she sighed. "You're right. It won't be easy, but maybe we can find moments when we can be ourselves, even if it's just for a short while. We'll have to be creative and work with the time we have."

Though it wasn't an ideal solution, Red knew they had to try. Their connection was too strong to ignore, and they would have to find a way to make it work. With determination and trepidation, they agreed to face the challenges together and see where their journey would take them.

"We're heading to the studio, right?" she asked.

"Will you be ready to leave in fifteen?"

She laughed. "I'll be ready in five." She took off running up the stairs and was back in moments dressed in jeans, heavy boots, and another polo with the Vortex logo.

As Red watched her, he couldn't help but reflect on how different Viv was from his usual type. He had previously gravitated towards women who could be described as "Party Barbie"—hot-blooded and high-maintenance. But there was something about Viv, with her no-nonsense attitude and "GI Jane" vibe, that he found irresistibly attractive.

He couldn't put his finger on it, but her strength and confidence drew him in like a magnet. Viv was the kind of woman who could hold her own in any situation, and he admired her for that. Perhaps it was the fact that she challenged his expectations and defied stereotypes that made her so intriguing. And the more time they spent together, the more he appreciated her unique blend of toughness and vulnerability.

"What do I do with Lucky?" He'd brought the dog with him everywhere he went thus far.

"Is it bring your kid to work day?" she asked.

He shook his head. "I think the noise will bother his ears."

"Then he gets to stay home and watch TV."

They settled Lucky in his kennel and turned on *Animal Planet* and went on their way. As Viv joined him, Red couldn't help but smile at his life's unexpected turn.

ONE HUNDRED DESIRES

RED PLAYED with the band at the studio as they laid down tracks for a new album. The whole time, his mind wasn't on the music. Thankfully no one noticed. His mind was on Viv, but he became more confused as he thought about her and their situation. If he'd had a mom, this would have been when he'd call and ask her advice, but he had no mom or influential female in his life. He needed to talk to someone about the situation, someone who would understand the complexities of their relationship. As he took a break, he decided to confide in Cameron. He trusted her judgment and hoped that she might offer some valuable advice on handling his growing desire for Viv without compromising her ability to protect him.

He picked up his phone and dialed her, his heart racing as he waited for her to answer. "Hey, Cam, it's Red. Do you have a minute to talk?"

Silence filled endless seconds of space. "Red? What's going on?"

He hesitated for a moment, unsure of where to begin. "It's about Viv," he finally admitted, his voice barely above a whisper. "I think I'm falling for her."

Cameron didn't hold back her shock. "Are you crazy? You know she's my sister-in-law! And you two are working together."

"I know, but—"

"This is a disaster waiting to happen."

Red took a deep breath, determined to make her understand. "Cam, I know it sounds insane, but it's different than anything I've ever felt. I can't help it, and I need some advice on how to navigate this."

"You want advice? Walk away, or Val will bury you."

"That's the thing. I can't walk away."

Cameron sighed. "Alright, Red, but you need to be

prepared to face her brother. And take it slow, and don't mess with her heart if yours isn't in it. When you get scared, and you think about doing something despicable and damaging, don't. You know, that's your MO. You do the hurting before someone can hurt you." He could almost see her shaking her head. "You're just repeating what's been done to you. You abandon your relationships before they can do it to you."

The words stunned him, but they didn't feel untrue. He'd been sabotaging his love life since he could remember. Was that the case? Was he protecting himself by hurting others?

He hung up the phone, feeling sad and guilty for all the hearts he had broken.

He returned to the recording booth. He promised Viv he would stay inside the locked studio while she ran a few errands, and he intended to keep his word.

When Viv returned, Red couldn't help but keep looking at her. Her eyes met his, and he saw a flicker of uncertainty in them, mirroring his own feelings.

When he had another break, he said, "I was feeling lost in my feelings for you, and I called Cameron for advice."

Viv's eyes widened in surprise. "You talked to Cameron? Red, she's a megaphone straight to Val."

Red winced. "I know, Viv. But what I feel is new, and I need help navigating it."

Viv sighed, a look of understanding crossing her face. "I get it, but you need to be prepared for my brother's reaction. He's extremely protective. I gather he's seen you at some of your worst, and he would never want me to compromise my own standards, professional or personal."

"Protecting was his line of work. That seems natural."

"Speaking of protection, I can't be your around-the-clock detail. So, I want you to meet Jackson." Viv stuck her head out the door and called for Jackson to come in.

In walked a tall, burly man with a serious expression. Red's eyes widened as he recognized him. "Aren't you the new bartender at Bishop's?"

Viv smiled, clearly pleased with herself. "And he's your new night security detail."

Red understood the implication of that all too well. He wouldn't get any more goodnight kisses unless he got them from Jackson—and Jackson was not his type. He couldn't help but chuckle at the thought, trying to picture himself leaning in for a peck on the cheek from the stoic, muscular man standing before him.

He turned to Viv with a playful grin. "Well, I hope Jackson here has a gentle touch. After all, I've grown quite accustomed to a certain level of tenderness in my nighttime routine."

Viv rolled her eyes, but her lips twitched with a suppressed smile. "Oh, don't worry. I'm sure Jackson can provide all the tenderness you need."

Seemingly unamused by their banter, Jackson crossed his arms and nodded solemnly. "I'll make sure you're well-protected, sir."

The lighthearted moment dissipated, but Red couldn't shake the feeling that things were about to get more interesting—not just because of the new security arrangements. She could remove herself from his presence, but that wouldn't stop him from kissing her; it just made it more challenging, and he liked a challenge.

"Happy to have you on board as part of my security detail."

As if on cue, the door to the recording studio slammed open, revealing a furious Val. His eyes narrowed as he glared at Red and Viv, his voice shaking with barely contained anger. "Viv, I told you Red would be a problem. You're here to protect him, not get drawn into his fake charm so he can devalue and try to control you."

Viv's eyes flashed with defiance as she positioned herself between Red and her brother. "You need to trust me to do my job and live my own life."

Val scoffed, his expression turning disdainful. "Trust you? I trusted you to keep your distance, to remember that you're a professional. But instead, you let yourself get involved with him. How can I trust you now?"

Red's heart ached at the hurt in Viv's eyes, and he couldn't stand by without defending her. He stepped forward, meeting Val's gaze with determination. "Val, your sister is an amazing bodyguard. She's shown only dedication and professionalism since we started working together. I've been blown away by everything she knows. She's amazing."

Val's anger shifted toward Red, and he took a menacing step toward him. "Stay out of this, Red. This is a family matter."

Before the situation could escalate further, Jackson stepped forward, placing a hand on Val's shoulder. "Let's take a step back and talk about this calmly. There's no need for things to get out of hand."

Val looked as though he wanted to argue, but the commanding presence of Jackson seemed to give him pause. He finally relented. His gaze turned to Viv. "Who is this guy?"

Viv's voice was steady and confident as she replied, "This is Jackson. He's the newest employee of Vortex Security."

Val's eyes widened, and he shook his head in disbelief.

"Vortex is a family business, Viv. You don't just bring in outsiders."

Viv met her brother's gaze, her voice firm but filled with a hint of sadness. "It was a family business, Val, until you left. We need help, and Jackson is more than qualified. He's here to ensure Red stays safe and give me some time off. I can't be effective if I'm on duty 24/7."

The tension in the room seemed to lessen, though the underlying issues remained unresolved. Val's expression softened, and he looked at his sister with concern and regret. "I know you're capable, Viv, but he's not good for you."

"This isn't the time or the place. We'll talk when I come back to your place tonight."

"You're coming home?"

"Now that we have Jackson for the night shift, I'll be staying at your home if that's alright. I haven't found mine yet." She turned to look over her shoulder at Red. "But I'm close."

Red felt joy at her words, though he tried his best to keep his expression neutral.

With the situation resolved for now, Val left, and Jackson promised to be at his house by nine. Red leaned in and whispered to Viv, "If you think leaving my home at night means you won't make it to my arms, you're wrong. I'm not giving up that easily. We will explore this thing between us, Viv. Don't fight it. It's inevitable."

"I'm not fighting." She reached up on tiptoes to kiss his cheek. "You already know I'm not cheap, and I'm making sure you know I'm not easy either. We've got work to do. Lots, and it doesn't start in your bed."

CHAPTER SEVENTEEN

Viv stood on the porch of Red's home ready to hand off her charge, her heart churning with the conflicting emotions that had been simmering throughout the day. Her green eyes flickered between the two men before her, both tall and alluring but radiating entirely different energies. Red, with his tousled brown hair and searing blue eyes, carried an air of "take me as I am" confidence that made him so incredibly sexy. Every woman wants to feel that way about themselves but without a glass or two of wine, most spend more time overthinking their flaws. Red knew just how to free them of those inhibitions by accepting himself and therefore any woman just as she was. It was natural, not contrived. For his faults he did not lack empathy or passion, and he was surprisingly easy-going. It was a very desirable combination. What's sexier than being appreciated just for who you are? Jackson, in contrast, stood steadfast, planted, and dependable with his military haircut and sharp laser-focused eyes scanning the yard's perimeter. He was strong and oozed character. Viv supposed that could be sexy too, but she at least didn't have to worry about any would-be groupie attacker seducing him – or trying to. While Red came off as all fun, Jackson was all business, like a leather briefcase with a combination lock. You'd have to really want to know what was inside to pick the lock. She knew he'd be a good fit for Red's security detail. Even without extensive personal security training, he was a natural at serving and protecting, and he had all the right skills and instincts.

"All right, Jackson, I'll be back at five in the morning," Viv said. She glanced at Red, searching for any emotion in his eyes, but he remained unreadable. "Take good care of our charge."

"You got it, Viv," Jackson replied with a nod, clapping a strong hand on her shoulder. "Have a good evening."

Viv hesitated, her gaze lingering on Red for just a moment longer. She could feel the warmth of his presence, his energy radiating like warm sand on a beach in the cool evening air. She shook her head, trying to clear her thoughts, and forced a smile onto her lips. "You too, Jackson."

With that, she turned away from the house, leaving Red and Jackson behind as she climbed into the Yukon and headed toward her brother's place.

The sky was a canvas of deep purples and blues, with a million stars filling the sky. It always fascinated her how the sky was the same in different locations, but the view was changed. In the city, you rarely see a sky like the one above because the noise of other lights dims its beauty. She considered that momentarily and wondered if that was the same for people like Cameron and Red. Their stars were so bright, but the noise of fame and fans often changed how they were perceived. Red had this awful reputation as being a womanizer, and she didn't doubt that he lived up to it, but was that who he truly was when you stripped it all away?

She was inclined to believe that Cameron was right—that Red simply didn't know how to love and hadn't afforded himself time to learn. The most enlightened and loving men like Val still behave as though relationships are self-sustaining, not realizing even rock gardens get weeds. How could someone like Red know better? Red wasn't only who people said he was; he was more. At least he seemed like he wanted to be more. She had to believe that if Cameron had fallen in love with him, Red had finer qualities than being good in bed. And she wouldn't consider finding out how good he could make her body feel until she had peeled back the layers of the man to see who he truly was. The image people project on you and the messages that come with it too often shape who someone becomes, and Red was pigeon-holed into fulfilling a rock and roll image with lots of poor messages. All she had to do was listen to the echo of her brother's voice, who told her that Red was no good, a seducer of women and a cheat. He may have been all those things, but her biggest question was, is he more? And the answer she heard in her heart was yes.

Twenty minutes later, she pulled into the driveway of her brother's cabin and slid out of the SUV. She had stopped noticing how big the car was for her. After inhaling the fresh scent of pine and the earthy aroma of damp soil, she knew she couldn't put off this conversation with Val any longer. As much as she wanted to avoid the confrontation, she also yearned for a resolution. At thirty-two, she was more than capable of making her own decisions and intended to make that clear to Val.

She noticed the warm, golden glow of light streaming from the windows. The cozy, log-built structure stood in stark contrast to, but in harmony with, the wild, untamed forest that surrounded it, offering a sense of security and familiarity. The sound of soft laughter drifted from within, and her heart ached at the thought of her niece, Natalie, and how much she longed for a family of her own—a place where she belonged.

Steeling herself for the conversation ahead, Viv rapped her knuckles against the wooden door. Almost immediately, it swung open, revealing her brother, Val, his rugged features softening as he took in her tired expression.

"Hey, Viv." He moved aside to let her enter. "How's everything going with the protection detail?"

"All's well," she replied, her voice steady despite the turmoil brewing inside her. "But we need to talk."

He frowned, concern etching lines into his brow. The interior was warm and inviting, the walls adorned with family photos and mementos that spoke of a life well-lived. Viv's gaze fell on a picture of her brother and Cameron, their arms wrapped around each other as they stood in front of their cabin, the epitome of love and happiness. She swallowed the lump in her throat, her chest tightening with a mixture of envy and longing.

"What's going on, Viv?" he asked, his voice gentle as he closed the door behind her.

"Where's Cameron?"

He nodded toward the hallway. "Changing the baby."

Viv sighed, running a hand through her blonde hair as she paced the length of the living room. "It's about Red. I know you disapprove of him, but I need you to understand that I can make my own decisions. I'm thirty-two, not a little girl anymore. And I think you need to consider how much of what you feel about Red is something you're projecting given his history with someone you love so deeply."

His eyes widened, and he crossed his arms over his

chest. "Viv, I just worry about you. You know his reputation."

Before Viv could respond, Cameron appeared in the doorway with a knowing smile on her face. "Sounds like you two are having the same conversation we had earlier," she said, her gaze alternating eagerly between them. "Val, your sister is a grown woman. She's more than capable of making her own choices and clearly capable of running the company."

Viv couldn't help but smile at her sister-in-law's support, feeling a surge of gratitude for her understanding. "Thank you, Cam."

Val sighed, rubbing his hand over his face. "I know, I know. I just... I can't help but worry about you. You're my sister, and I want the best for you. And as for the company, I know you can run it, but I never expected you'd physically take my place on the team. I expected you to continue to do the security protocol and cyber stuff. I didn't leave to put you in danger. I left to take me out of it."

Viv walked over to her brother and placed a hand on his arm. "I've always been in danger. Each time we step out the door, it's dangerous. I don't have to be a bodyguard to be exposed to danger. It's on every road and in every building. Hell, I probably have a likelier chance of getting eaten by a bear in your backyard than I do getting hurt by stalker Sarah. Whether it's my personal or professional life, I need you to trust me to make my own decisions, even if you disagree with them."

As if on cue, Natalie grunted and turned to face Viv. "Looks like it's Auntie Viv's time." She reached out, and Cameron carefully placed the baby in her arms.

As she sat and stared down at her niece, she wondered if she would ever have a family, a home that radiated the same love and belonging as her brother's did. She knew that continuing her current path as a bodyguard might not afford her that opportunity, and it was a realization that both frightened and saddened her. Wasn't this professional freedom what she always wanted?

Val studied her for a long moment, his eyes searching hers, before finally nodding in agreement. "All right, Viv. You're right about it all. I'll do my best to back off. Just ... be careful, okay?"

With that, the tension in the room dissipated, and the family settled in for a peaceful evening together. Viv cherished the time spent with her brother, Cameron, and Natalie, knowing that these moments were a balm for her soul. And as she held her niece in her arms, she made a silent promise to herself. She would find a way to have it all —a career she loved, a family she adored, and a love that set her heart on fire.

As bedtime approached, Val rose and took Natalie, leaving her alone with Cameron. "Can I ask you something?" Viv took a seat across from her sister-in-law.

"Of course, Viv," Cameron replied, her warm smile inviting Viv to share her thoughts.

"Do you ever regret leaving Hollywood? Giving up your career to have a family?" Her voice cracked slightly with emotion.

Cameron took a moment to consider her response. "You know, when I won that Oscar, I said in my acceptance speech that you could have it all. But you can't really have it all if you want to enjoy what you've got. And at a point, what you want shifts. I have everything I want right here with Val and Natalie. And you as my sister."

She looked up at Cam and saw eyes filled with conviction and satisfaction. *Well, shit. I might be forced to rethink my life plan*, Viv thought.

"Leaving Hollywood was a difficult decision, but when I look at what I have now—Val, Natalie, this life we've built together—I know in my heart that it was the right choice. I've never been happier."

Viv listened intently, her mind swirling with the implications of Cameron's words. It was clear that she had a choice to make about her own path, and her heart pounded with the uncertainty of it all. For now, however, she would focus on the love and support surrounding her in that cozy cabin. As the evening evaporated into night, she and Cameron continued to share stories, laughter, and a growing sense of understanding.

Outside, an owl hooted, and Viv realized how exhausted she was. The emotions of the day had taken their toll on her.

Cameron offered a comforting smile. "Get some rest, Viv. You need it. And remember, whatever you decide about your future, we're here for you and love you."

"Can I ask you one more question?" Viv asked hesitantly. "I've been thinking about Red and the possibility of us dating. Given your past with him, is it weird that I'm considering it?"

Cameron cocked her head and looked forward with a thoughtful expression. "Viv, life isn't about dwelling on the past. It's about living in the present and looking forward to and shaping the future," she said softly. "Red and I had our time, but we've both moved on. What's important is that you follow your heart and do what makes you happy. If that's Red, then I say go for it. We all grow as people, and I'm sure he's not the same Red I knew and loved. I hope he's better for you. I accept some responsibility for what happened between us. It does take two to tango. While I can't condone most of his behavior as he tried in his way to hang on to me and our relationship, I can also see how I enabled and even inadvertently brought it on. What we thought was love was just both of us working through our obstacles on a journey to finding true love."

Viv listened intently, her mind racing again as she absorbed Cameron's words. At that moment, she experienced a profound sense of clarity.

Viv's heart swelled with appreciation as she embraced Cameron, whispering, "Thank you. Your support means more to me than you know."

Retreating to the guest room, Viv settled into the soft, welcoming bed. The familiar scent of the cabin's wooden walls and fresh mountain air filled her senses. Her thoughts drifted to Red, and she couldn't help but wonder what he was doing then. She knew she would have to confront her deepening feelings for him eventually, but for now, she allowed herself to be lulled to sleep by the gentle sounds of the night.

MORNING ARRIVED with the promise of a new day, and Viv awoke feeling refreshed and determined. As she readied herself to return to Red's house, she was filled with excitement and anticipation. She dressed and showered and said goodbye to her brother.

As she stepped out of the cabin, the crisp morning air greeted her, and she took a deep breath, feeling a renewed sense of purpose. She knew the road ahead wouldn't be easy, but with her loved ones by her side and the strength of her determination, she was ready to face whatever life had in store for her. The journey to herself had taken a sharp and unexpected turn. It was unsettling but also strangely welcome.

With a final wave goodbye to Cameron, who stood in the doorway cradling a still-sleepy Natalie, Viv climbed into her Yukon and drove. The sun was cresting over the mountains, bathing the world in a golden light, and Viv felt a sense of hope blossoming in her heart.

The quiet serenity of the early morning drive gave Viv the perfect opportunity to reflect on her life and her choices. The beauty of the landscape around her seemed to intensify her thoughts, allowing her to see her situation with a fresh set of eyes. She loved the quote she had seen from a French author that the real voyage of life had to do not with seeking new landscapes but with finding new eyes. Most of her life choices and epiphanies happened when she was in one place, not while she was gallivanting around exotic destinations.

Viv couldn't help but contemplate her future as the road stretched before her. She had dedicated herself to a bodyguard's high-stakes, high-stress life, but had she ever truly considered what she was sacrificing in the process? Had she even ever considered the alternatives?

The time spent with her brother's family had awakened a deep longing within her—a longing for the warmth and stability of a home and family of her own. She realized that continuing down the path she had chosen might not allow her the opportunity to fulfill those dreams. The demands of her job, the constant travel, and the unpredictability of her schedule were not conducive to building the kind of life she had not considered she could have but now craved.

This moment of clarity left Viv feeling both vulnerable and hopeful. She blossomed to the possibility of change, of leaving her current frenetic life behind in search of something more fulfilling. She knew people appreciated her, but running and growing the family business was never going to hug her or give her a kiss goodnight or a family of her own. And as she considered this potential new direction, her thoughts inevitably turned to Red. There was no evidence that he was "future" material, at least not based on his past. But aren't we all more than our pasts?

The connection she felt with Red was undeniable, and the thought of exploring a future together excited and terrified her. What was the security protocol for love? For preventing a broken heart? Although he made it clear he wanted them to explore their feelings too, they certainly weren't at the place where they'd be making life commitments. Still, both of them wanting something more from each other seemed like more than half the battle at this point. They could be thinking about the future soon if things kept moving them in the right direction.

CHAPTER EIGHTEEN

Over the next few weeks, Red found himself falling deeper for Viv. Their time together was filled with laughter, heartfelt conversations, and stolen kisses. The more he got to know her, the more he realized what an extraordinary woman she truly was. She was a force of nature. He marveled at how she'd survived six brothers and managed not just to hold her own but exceed all of their expectations. Her need to be resilient somehow never dampened her warmth, skewed her character, or quelled her laughter. In fact, Viv's playful nature and quick wit kept him off his guard. He really didn't know how to sweep her off her feet, so he reconciled himself to just being himself and letting things unfold. Viv's spirited personality and her smile were an elixir to his soul. His world seemed to grow brighter and more vibrant with her light by his side.

One sunny afternoon, they took Lucky for a walk down Main Street. The sound of the dog's nails clicking on the pavement blended harmoniously with the distant chatter of people going about their day. Red breathed in the crisp mountain air, noticing the faint scent of freshly baked goods wafting from the local bakery. Viv's hand in his felt warm and comforting, and he stole a quick kiss from her as they walked.

They stopped at the cozy diner they had grown fond of during their time in town. Red held the door open for Viv, and they were greeted by the friendly smile of Maisey, who knew their order by heart and allowed dogs as long as they told her Lucky was an emotional support pet and promised he wouldn't lift his leg on the booth. She knew he was just a mutt and a rescue, but she didn't care. He was family, and family was always welcome at the diner.

They settled into their usual booth, contentment wrapped around him like a warm blanket. The buzz of conversation, the smell of sizzling bacon, and the warmth of Viv's thigh pressed against his combined to create a comforting atmosphere that felt like home.

Over their usual hearty breakfast, they shared stories from their pasts, both the happy and the challenging. He listened intently as she spoke, marveling again at the humility with which her resilience and strength came through. He felt grateful that fate, no matter how unsettling, had brought them together.

After enjoying their usuals, they continued their stroll through town and found themselves at B's Bakery. The sweet aroma of butter and sugar washed over them as they entered. Red looked down at Viv, her eyes sparkling with excitement as she surveyed the mouthwatering display of cookies, muffins, and brownies. They chose an assortment and sat at the table to share a brownie.

"Have you ever wished for anything?" Viv looked up at the board that was labeled The Wishing Wall.

"I've wished for many things in my life but nothing from here."

"You should make a wish." She took a pen from the hanging bin and a yellow sticky note.

Lucky yelped as if concurring with Viv. "What would I wish for? For the first time ever, I feel like I've got everything I need."

"Do you? What about this brownie?"

He took a bite of the turtle brownie and let the flavors of caramel, chocolate, and nuts meld together. They were paired perfectly with just enough sweetness, salt, and bitterness to make them delicious and addictive. He realized life wasn't all that different from the brownie as he thought about the chemistry of the blended flavors. Some things looked like they went together, like a musician and a movie star, but it wasn't the best combination when you opened the packages and tried to mix them together. Finding the right ingredients for success takes a lot of experimentation and often takes a lot of time. He and Viv had chemistry. Did they have all the right ingredients for the perfect mix? She seemed like a perfect mix for him. She knew about his past but didn't hold it against him. She knew what it was like to be an underdog and fight to the top and have to keep fighting to stay there. Their battles were different, but battles that shaped them, nonetheless. He battled inner demons and feelings of worthlessness. She battled society's unspoken rules and her family. He could have included her diminutive size, but that didn't even occur to him. He saw Viv as tall and mighty.

"There are things I want that I don't have. They're probably things I need, but I'm unaware of their necessity and value." He reached down and petted Lucky. "Like this guy. I needed him but wouldn't have taken him in without your prodding."

She laughed. "It's not like I gave you much choice. I screamed 'stop,' and you did."

"I'm good at following directions. I've done everything you asked, right?" He wasn't usually good with rules but wanted to make things easier for Viv. Besides, resistance seemed useless, and he didn't want to risk losing her before they'd had a chance to get to know each other.

"You've been an excellent client."

"And you've been a great bodyguard. I haven't had a single trespasser since I hired you."

"The security system helps, and you're never alone."

"True." He didn't know if it was time to broach the subject, but it needed to be said. "Do you think I still need a security detail?" He didn't want her to think he was firing her, but Viv had stringent rules about fraternization. While she let him kiss her, there was no way she would let their relationship progress, and he wanted more—needed more. "I default to your wisdom and experience, but Sarah hasn't been seen anywhere near me since your rental car disaster."

"True, but we've made it harder for her to get in or destroy what she doesn't want to see, like another woman's vehicle in front of your house."

Viv paid Jackson to return her car and borrowed her brother's to get back and forth. For the most part, they took his truck everywhere which made him feel needed. The problem with Cameron was that she had never needed him. Everything he could give her, she could get herself or get from her fans, but Viv seemed to need him as much as he did her.

"Do you think the threat is over?"

She sighed. "I think with the type of work you do and your reputation, the threat is forever, but I can understand why you'd want to cut me loose."

He reached across the table and took her hands. "Cutting you loose is the last thing on my mind. Getting closer is what I want, and that isn't going to happen while we have a professional relationship."

She pointed to the sticker and pen. "Then make a wish."

"And you're going to grant it? The wish I'd make isn't the kind of thing I can put on a public board."

"Oh my." She took a bite of brownie and chewed slowly, but Red could see she was trying to figure out what he would wish for. "Give me a try."

That was his wish, but he wouldn't be so base when he asked and didn't want just a try. He was hedging for the long term. While he wasn't ready to offer forever, he wanted more than a single night or two. So, he took the note and penned his heartfelt wish, and handed it to Viv.

As she read it, he watched her for a reaction, but Viv was wearing her best poker face. "You want all of this?"

"That's only a start."

She cocked her head. "Wow. I imagined your wish would look like a cross between a list of college courses and a hot romance novel—chemistry, shared passions, history, the simmering climax of joining our bodies and souls. I wasn't expecting this." She stared at him and nodded, and he thought it was a done deal until she said, "I need some assurances first."

Was she asking for forever and a ring? That never seemed to go well for him. "Umm, what kind of assurances are you thinking of? Guaranteed multiple orgasms? Breakfast in bed? I have to learn pole dancing?"

Viv gave him that soul-affirming smile he had hoped to elicit. "It's not really what I need; it's what we should do to make sure expectations don't fly away and take us somewhere we don't want to go emotionally or otherwise, and I need to feel sure there are no more threats against you. Plus, I think a thorough check-up with the doc is probably in order."

"Oh, I can do that. By the way, I may not have played it safe as far as women were concerned, but I always played safely. In addition to the stalkers there are fans who bank on paternity suits as well. Looking at it all, I've been fortunate and more careful than you'd expect. I didn't earn all of my reputation, but sex and the idea that I'm having it all the time sells," he laughed. "As far as expectations go, my only desire is to know you, to hold you, to discover you and to explore with you what we could be together, whatever that becomes. I want us to grow and learn about how to love each other."

She laughed. "You look pale. Oh my gosh. Did you think I wanted to march you down the aisle?" She rolled her eyes. "No worries. It's far too late for either of us to be virgin brides. I'm not looking for a wedding just yet. Besides, my mom was not in the 'why should he buy the cow if he gets the milk free' camp. She always told me to try it before you buy it and make sure your bull is hung the way you like. Doesn't matter how many cows he can milk if he doesn't satisfy you."

Red almost blushed. "I already like your mom." He considered the Armstrong family and wondered why Viv's mom wasn't there already, seeing as her brother just had a baby. "I would have thought she'd be here."

"Oh, she's coming soon, and they might never get rid of her. Natalie is the first and only grandchild. If anyone thinks my mom is leaving after she arrives, they are nuts. I saw some plans on Val's table for a cabin they will build across the lake."

"Your brother used the same company I did. Cooper Construction could have it up and ready in weeks. They use these cool kits, and they are earth friendly."

She looked at him strangely. "You never cease to amaze me. A musician and a tree hugger."

"Hey, we must preserve what's good in the world."

Viv looked at the note and tucked it in her pocket. She nodded, a soft smile on her face. "You're right. To take care of the people we love, we do need to take care of the world we live in. Speaking of which, I think it's time for us to review your safety protocol again."

He wanted to groan because Viv drilled into him all the safety measures he'd need from here until eternity, but he knew that once she signed off on this job, she'd no longer be his bodyguard and could simply be his.

They headed back to his house, where Viv took the time to explain the ins and outs of the security system she had installed, again. She showed him how to lock the doors, set the alarms, monitor the surveillance cameras, and enter a panic code. She reiterated that working in fear made the mind unclear. If he were ever in a dangerous situation he should slow down and consider everything he knew before he laid out a plan. Red listened attentively, grateful for her expertise and dedication to his safety. When she was finished, she held out her hand and shook his. "It was nice doing business with you." She rose from the couch, and he thought she would leave. "Are you leaving?"

She shook her head. "Can I borrow a shirt?"

"You can have anything you want." He meant it.

She walked away and came back a few minutes later, no longer wearing her Vortex uniform. She was now in one of his Indigo T-shirts and never looked better. Unless he compared her to the day she came out wearing his boxers and a T-shirt. That was better.

She sat on the couch next to him, snuggled into his side, and pointed to the old guitar in the corner. "Have you ever written a song for a woman?"

Red glanced at the guitar, chuckling before looking back at Viv. "You know, I've never actually written a song for a woman," he admitted, an amused smile on his lips. "I've always been terrified of the idea. Can you imagine being like Eric Clapton, singing 'Layla' for decades after he and Pattie Boyd broke up? Or like Gwen Stefani, forever belting out 'Don't Speak' about her ex-bandmate?"

Viv laughed, nodding in understanding. "Oh, I see what you mean. That would be quite the emotional torture."

"Yeah," Red continued, grinning. "I mean, imagine having to sing about someone long gone, night after night, year after year? It's like a never-ending emotional roller coaster. No, thank you!"

Viv joined in his laughter, clearly enjoying the light-hearted conversation. "Well, you do have a point there."

"But," Red added, his gaze lingering on the guitar, "I've got to admit, there's something about you, Viv, that makes music inside me. I sing about you in my head all day long. It's strange, but I feel like I could write a whole album about you and never get tired of singing it."

Viv blushed, a playful grin spreading across her face. "Really? Well, I suppose I should feel honored, but I'll pass on the breakup anthem. Instead, I'll take the memories we make together."

As they sat together, their love story unfolding in the quiet moments and stolen glances, Red couldn't help but feel inspired. And while he didn't voice it, he knew deep down that the love they were building was more profound than any song could ever capture. But that didn't mean he wouldn't keep the idea of writing a song for Viv tucked away for a later day.

When the night grew late, and they lay on the couch dozing in each other's arms, he knew he had to send her home to her brother's before he begged her to stay. When he finally made love to her, he wanted it to be perfect. She deserved candles and flowers and shrimp cocktail and baked Alaska. Viv made it clear that she wanted more, and he was sure he wanted to give it.

Maybe that was his problem all along. Maybe he should have wanted more. Maybe he should have demanded more. For the first time, he felt like he deserved it.

CHAPTER NINETEEN

Now that the security detail was done, Viv found herself with an abundance of time and freedom to explore Aspen Cove with Red. They spent their days wandering the picturesque streets, visiting Red's friends and bandmates, and making memories that made putting off romance worthy of the wait, beautiful moments that would remind her what it meant to love and live.

One especially beautiful day, they decided to hike up to a nearby waterfall, a local spot several townspeople had recommended. The trail was lined with tall, majestic trees, their branches swaying gently in the breeze. The sound of rushing water grew louder with each step, and soon, they found themselves standing before the breathtaking cascade of water, the mist kissing their faces and filling the air with a refreshing coolness.

"I can't believe we've never been here before," Viv marveled, her eyes wide with wonder as she took in the beauty of what nature made.

Red wrapped his arm around her, pulling her close as they stood together, watching the water tumble over and down the rocks. "It's the perfect place for a picnic." Red let his backpack slide to the ground next to where Lucky sat, panting. The dog had nearly doubled in size in the weeks since they'd found him. Red was having the time of his life teaching him new things like sitting and playing dead. He was like a proud parent who would tell anyone willing to listen about their dog's intelligence. The funny thing was he had started telling everyone that Lucky was theirs, not his, which filled her with a sense of warmth and belonging.

"Here, buddy." Red filled a collapsible bowl with water for Lucky, who lapped it up happily.

Viv spread the blanket on the soft grass while Red unpacked the basket filled with their favorite sandwiches, fruits, and a bottle of wine. Lucky settled down beside them, wagging his tail and panting happily.

"So beautiful," Viv murmured, her eyes fixed on the vibrant colors of the rainbow arching over the waterfall. She turned to Red with a curious expression. "Do you think there's a meaning behind rainbows?"

Red thought momentarily then shared the stories he knew about rainbows as symbols of hope, love, and good fortune. He also mentioned the Irish legend of the pot of gold at the end of the rainbow. Viv listened intently, her eyes sparkling with interest.

"Maybe for us," Viv said, her voice growing soft and tender, "the rainbow could symbolize the journey we've taken together. It's like the treasure we've found in each other."

Red's eyes grew misty as he smiled at her. "I like that idea."

They sat together, hands entwined, as they watched the rainbow slowly fade, leaving the memory of its fleeting beauty behind.

"Maybe we should have wished on the rainbow."

"I already have a wish out there that hasn't been granted." His chuckle was quickly silenced when, without warning, he pressed his lips to her neck right where her pulse beat against them. He opened his mouth and let his tongue blaze a path of heat that spread everywhere. Everything in her body misfired. Not a single nerve ending was functioning correctly. Every pleasure point stood up and said *pick me*, hoping to be the next stop on his journey. Warm kisses trailed from her neck to her ear to the hollow above her collarbone. He may have only kissed her there, but she felt it everywhere. Even her toes curled inside her shoes. She wanted so much more.

Red hadn't pressured her for anything, which was unexpected. He'd been loving and patient, and it felt like the right moment to bring their shared wish for joy to fruition.

She pulled out the sticky note she kept in her back pocket. She liked to look at it and dream about a day when what he wanted could come true.

"It's about time for wishes to come true." She unfolded the yellow note and handed it back to him. She watched as he read over the words he'd written and wondered if he still wanted what they said.

Let me have one night, and I'll show you that forever will never be enough.

"Are you ready for this?"

She nodded, and he kissed her. This time the kiss was a raging fire that melted into her very bones. She felt at once intoxicated with desire and unbearably hot. His touch stirred a thousand different feelings within her, and she welcomed them all as his lips moved against hers. She'd never leave his bed if he made love the way he kissed.

He deepened the kiss and wrapped her in his arms as if

he was protecting her from the outside world, which seemed funny since she was the one who had been looking after him all this time. The kiss seemed to last an eternity and yet felt too short at the same time. When he finally pulled away, she felt like she was standing on the edge of a cliff, swaying between pleasure and fear but ready to go anywhere he wanted to take her. If he had asked her to jump, she might have because, after that kiss, she knew he'd catch her.

"How about a date with all the bells and whistles?"

She lifted a brow. "What do all the bells and whistles include?"

His blue eyes took on a stormy, sexy look. "Everything."

Goosebumps covered her skin. "Everything?"

"I'm not holding anything back." He lifted to a sitting position and reached into his wallet, where he pulled out a piece of paper that had been folded in half two times. "You asked for this." He handed it to her.

When she unfolded it, she realized it was a note from Doc confirming his health. He'd given her everything she'd asked for. She could get everything she wanted.

"When?" Her breath came out in a whisper. Not a fearful voice but a can't-catch-her-breath-from-anticipation sound.

"Tomorrow night. I'll pick you up."

"I can't wait." She felt drunk with anticipation.

He kissed her gently before starting to pack up their things. "You'll have to. Shall I get you back so you can have Aunt Viv time with Natalie before she goes to bed?"

"She'd like that."

"What would you like?"

She sighed. "Another kiss."

He kissed her like tomorrow was a year from now, and

this kiss would have to sustain them. When he pulled away, she only wanted more. A thrill raced down her spine because tomorrow came with the promise of everything.

They walked down the path holding hands. Lucky happily trotted behind them. At the car, she caught a glimpse of something in the woods but couldn't see anything when she tried to focus. Though she wasn't on duty, she was always on guard.

"What's wrong?" Red must have felt her tense.

"Nothing. It was probably an animal or the breeze moving a branch." She looked around once more and let the feeling that something was wrong pass. "It's nothing."

He opened the door and helped her inside the truck. "And you're everything."

When they reached her brother's cabin, he helped her out and told Lucky he'd be right back. The pup pressed his face to the window and watched them walk away.

"You don't have to walk me to my door."

"Oh yes, I do. Besides, I need to talk to your brother."

She narrowed her eyes. "About what?"

The door opened, and Val filled the enormous space.

"Just the man I'm looking for." Red nodded toward the lake. "Can I have a moment of your time?"

"Are you sure that's wise?"

Red shook his head. "Nope, but it's necessary."

Val moved aside, but when Viv stepped up next to him, she said, "Don't kill him because we have a date tomorrow."

She walked into the house and made a beeline for her niece, who was on a blanket on the floor, looking up at several toys hanging above her head.

"Hey, princess." She scooped her up, having become more familiar with babies over the last several weeks. She even watched her niece one night while her brother and

Cameron ran into Copper Creek for supplies. She'd panicked a bit when Natalie got fussy, but a little snuggling and a walk around the living room put her right to sleep.

"You're back," Cameron said as she appeared from the hall.

"I am, and don't try to steal her from me just yet. You can have her when she gets fussy or pees."

Cameron laughed. "You sound like a grandparent. It's what they like best about their kids having kids. You get all the good parts and get to hand them back when the unpleasant parts come up."

"Pretty much all the parts have been pleasant. Everyone would have a dozen kids if all kids were like your daughter."

Cameron laughed. "No one could afford a dozen. Have you seen the diapers we go through?"

"I have." Viv kissed the little cherub on the forehead and placed her back on the blanket to stare at the stars and colored rainbows that hung about her head. "I need your help."

Cameron smiled. "Does this have to do with Red?" She rubbed her tired eyes. "I may have dated him, but it was a whirlwind, and we rushed past all the stuff we should have paid attention to. I'm not the best one to offer advice about him."

In all her life, Viv never imagined that she'd be falling in love with a man who had been engaged to her brother's wife. They lived in a twisted world, but it was her world, and she'd have to get used to it. "I'm not looking for advice about Red. I'm looking for advice on how to dress for our first real date."

Cameron looked at her strangely. "But you've been seeing him for over a month."

"Not really seeing him in the dating sense. The first month I was working for him. I never mix business with pleasure." She blushed because that was kind of a lie with Red. "Okay, I'll confess to kissing him, but it never went beyond that."

Cameron's mouth fell open. "Never?"

"No. And since then, we've been taking things slowly. I'm talking slug speed ahead. Sloths at the zoo. Maybe he learned something from you because we are paying attention to all the important things like open and honest communication, our likes and dislikes, our shared and individual expectations. Honestly, some days it's like full on therapy, but taking our time has brought us closer than either of us have ever felt to someone. The only time I've seen him naked was when he called me to help him with the Sarah problem."

"Wait. You mean that since you've stopped working together, you still haven't—"

"Nope, but tomorrow, we have a date. It's a real date with all the bells and whistles, and I'd like to wear something nicer than jeans and a T-shirt."

"Wow, he has changed. He's investing in you."

"We are invested in each other. And I think he's investing in himself too."

"I'm so glad. I always knew Red was a good guy; I just wasn't the right girl to bring it out in him, and neither of us was ready for what we thought everyone wanted from us. It was stupid. I'm so glad he found you." She picked up the baby. "Come with me. I've got you covered."

Inside Cameron's bedroom was a walk-in closet as big as a New York City apartment. Viv didn't know what she could pull together. It wasn't like they were similar in build. Cameron was far taller than her, but she went straight for a little black dress. "This should work. It's a mini-dress on me, so it should come mid-thigh or below for you." She went to the wall of shoes. "You look a seven. While your boots would make a statement, I don't see them finishing off the look." She pulled a pair of gemstone-adorned flats from the shelf. "I used to love these, but I swear my feet grew half a size with Natalie. Try them on."

She slipped out of her clothes and into the dress, which fit like it was made for her. And the shoes were a perfect fit as well. "I love them."

"I'll help with your makeup and hair."

Viv smiled. "I never had a big sister to show me stuff."

"You do now."

In the living room, she heard the sound of her brother and Red. She quickly changed her clothes and dashed to Red to ensure he was okay.

"Everyone fine?"

Val smiled and nodded. "Your boyfriend wanted to assure me he had the best intentions for you. He agreed that if he ever broke your heart, I could murder him and feed him to the wild animals in the forest."

She looked up into Red's eyes. "Wow, that's some commitment."

Red put his arm around her. "I don't plan on ever being bear bait."

She walked him to his car, and he kissed her. The slow, soft kiss left her wishing it was tomorrow.

"I'll pick you up at six," he said.

"I'll be waiting right here." She returned to the cabin and watched him drive away. When she went back inside, she approached her brother, pressing her hand to his forehead.

"What are you doing?" Val asked.

"Checking you for fever because if you're sick, then I'm exposed, and there's no way I'm missing that date tomorrow."

"You won't miss the date."

"Have you changed your mind about Red?"

Her brother smiled. "Not yet, but I told him I'll use him for target practice if he does anything that makes you unhappy."

She laughed. "Don't forget; I can outshoot you. Red doesn't have to worry about you. He has to worry about me."

"Good point." Her brother rose and walked down the hallway.

She went to her room, anticipating her date with Red.

CHAPTER TWENTY

Red paced around his living room, occasionally stopping to straighten a cushion or adjust a picture frame. The house needed to be perfect for his date with Viv tonight. He'd spent the entire day cleaning, and now everything was spotless. But he couldn't shake the nagging feeling that he'd forgotten something important.

"Alright, Lucky," Red said. "I think we've got everything. Wine, candles, flowers, shrimp cocktail, prime rib, and baked Alaska for dessert." He ticked off the items on his fingers, just to be sure. "What do you think, buddy? Am I missing anything?"

Lucky tilted his head and barked as if to reassure his owner that everything was in order. Red sighed, trying to shake off his nerves. "Tonight might be the beginning of forever, so everything must be spot-on."

With a reassuring wag of his tail, Lucky seemed to understand. He followed Red around the house as the final preparations were made. Red placed a lighter by the candles so he could create a warm, romantic ambiance. He carefully arranged the bouquet he'd picked up earlier from the Corner Store, making sure each bloom was visible and adding a touch of color to the table.

Red plated the shrimp cocktail garnished with parsley and a flourish of lemon slices cut so thinly they curled, double checking the presentation was just right before he placed it back in the refrigerator. The prime rib was cooking to perfection—he'd left plenty of time for it to sit before carving it later on, so the juices would redistribute nicely. The overstuffed baked potatoes were almost done, and the baked Alaska, which he made from scratch, sat in the freezer, the kitchen torch at the ready to set it alight for the flambee extravaganza at the end of their meal, caramelizing the meringue enveloping the cake and ice cream. He thought with a bit of satisfaction that he had outdone himself this time.

After one last check to guarantee everything was just right, Red hurried down the hallway to get dressed. He'd chosen a crisp white shirt and a pair of black slacks, wanting to look his best for Viv. As he buttoned up his shirt, he caught a glimpse of himself in the mirror. "Not too shabby," he muttered, giving himself a nod of approval.

Lucky, who had followed him, let out an approving bark. Red smiled, grateful for the vote of confidence. "Thanks, buddy. Now, all we need is Viv. Shall we go and get her?"

They headed to his truck, ready to sweep her off her feet with the romantic night he'd planned. The anticipation hung in the air, a palpable energy that promised to deliver memories worth making and the moments of bliss they'd been dreaming of and waiting for. Red couldn't wait a nanosecond longer. Viv wouldn't mind if he were a minute or two early, right?

Red and Lucky climbed into the truck. The drive to

Val's cabin was one that Red had come to enjoy. The winding mountain road took them through the woods, where the trees stood tall like ancient guardians, their branches intertwined overhead as if holding hands.

Red couldn't help but appreciate the beauty of the forest. The sun filtered through the canopy, casting dappled patterns of light and shadow on the ground below. It felt as though nature was guiding him to Viv, the golden beams of sunlight illuminating his path. As he drove, he noticed the wildlife that called these woods home—squirrels scampering across branches, and birds flitting from tree to tree, their songs filling the air with a chorus of melody.

Lucky, too, seemed to enjoy the ride. He sat in the passenger seat, his nose pressed against the window, taking in the sights and smells of the woods. Occasionally, he'd perk up, his ears twitching as he caught the scent of a deer or rabbit hidden among the trees. Red smiled at his canine companion, knowing that Lucky was just as excited about welcoming Viv as he was.

As they continued their journey, Red couldn't help but think about what the future might hold for him and Viv. The connection they shared had grown deeper with each passing day, and it felt like they were on the cusp of something that could actually last. Hope effervesced through him like never before. It was a strange cocktail of giddiness, solemness, and love. Viv was the one he had waited for, literally. He felt deep in his heart that tonight would begin a new chapter in their lives, one filled with love and happiness in ways he'd never considered possible.

Finally, the truck rounded a bend, and the cabin appeared. It was nestled among the trees, a cozy sanctuary that blended seamlessly with its surroundings. Red pulled up to the front, excitement coursing through his veins like a sixteen-year-old taking Taylor Swift to a prom. This was it—the moment he'd been preparing for.

He glanced over at Lucky, who was wagging his tail in anticipation. "Alright, buddy, let's go get our girl." Together, they exited the truck and made their way to the cabin door, the sun's rays dancing through the trees as if to cheer them on. The beginning of forever awaited them, and Red was ready to embrace it with open arms.

Viv opened the cabin door, and Red's breath caught in his throat. She stood there, wearing a black dress that hugged her curves in all the right places. The hemline flirted just above her knees, showcasing her toned legs. Her black flats, adorned with sparkling rhinestones, caught the sunlight, making her feet shimmer with each subtle movement. It was like Oz with only magic and no evil witches—enchanted.

Red had never seen Viv dressed like this before. He was used to seeing her in jeans and a T-shirt, her hair tucked away beneath a ball cap. Looking so elegant and alluring, this vision of her left him momentarily speechless. The transformation was stunning, and he couldn't help but stare, entirely captivated by her beauty.

Viv smiled, a hint of mischief in her eyes as she took in Red's reaction. "Well, hello there," she said, her voice soft and inviting. "You clean up pretty well yourself."

Red blinked, snapping back to reality. "Uh, yeah, thank you," he stammered, suddenly self-conscious in his attire. "You look... I mean, you're... Wow, Viv, you're breathtaking."

Her cheeks flushed a rosy pink at his compliment, and she glanced down at her dress. "I thought it was about time I ditched the jeans and cap for something a bit more...

special," she said, her eyes meeting his again. "Seems like tonight's the perfect occasion for it."

Red couldn't have agreed more. The sight of Viv standing in her dress made his heart race and his palms sweat. It was all he could do not to whisk her into his arms and carry her back to her bedroom. Suddenly, shrimp cocktail, prime rib, and baked Alaska were more foreplay than he thought he could handle. *Get a hold of yourself, man! You've come this far. You can wait a while longer to show this gorgeous woman how much you love her.* He wanted tonight to be a night to remember, not one where Val would beat, tar, and feather him.

"Shall we?" he asked, extending his arm for her to take. Viv reached behind the door to grab her bag before she looped her hand around the cradle of his arm, the warmth of her body sending shivers through his whole body.

As they climbed into Red's truck, Lucky claimed his usual spot on Viv's lap. Red glanced at her before starting the engine, still awestruck by her beauty. With a warm smile, Viv playfully rolled her eyes and gently nudged him. "Come on, let's get this show on the road." Red loved that she didn't even think about dog hair, even when she was all dressed up.

With a chuckle, Red pulled away from the cabin and onto the winding mountain road leading them back to his home.

The drive seemed to take no time. They arrived, and Red lifted Viv out of the truck just so he could wrap himself around her, even for a minute. Viv giggled like a child who had not a care in the world. Lucky bounded out after them, eager to join in on the festivities. As they walked towards the front door, excitement and nerves danced in Red's heart and stomach. He hoped that the night would live up to Viv's expectations. He had set the bar high and did not want to disappoint the person who'd become so integral to how he now saw himself—he was someone who could love, wanted to love, and deserved to love and be loved. It was ecstasy just to revel in the closeness and the bond he and Viv had built just by getting to know one another.

Inside, Red led Viv to the dining room, where the table was set with elegant place settings and the bouquet he had arranged earlier. Viv gasped. "Red, this is so beautiful. You've outdone yourself. Oh my gosh, the house smells like the finest restaurant and looks like a magazine cover."

His nerves eased by her reaction, Red couldn't help but beam with pride. "I wanted tonight to be perfect for you, Viv."

As Viv settled into her seat, she closed her eyes and breathed deeply. "Is that garlic I smell?"

"I made prime rib and covered it with spices, including garlic."

"It smells amazing. I'm starving and could eat a calf by myself."

"I've got you covered. I ordered three times what the butcher recommended." He'd grown accustomed to her appetite and had purchased an eight-pound roast to be safe.

"I can't wait to taste everything you've prepared," she said excitedly.

"I hope I remembered everything you put on your date list."

She narrowed her eyes. "I never made a list."

"Let's start and see if you remember."

The champagne cork burst from the bottle like a rocket, making a popping sound that could mean only a good time was ahead and there was something to celebrate.

The dinner began with the shrimp cocktail. They

weren't the tiny shrimp you'd find in the grocery store, but super jumbo prawns he overnighted from the Gulf of Mexico like they serve in the finest steak houses in New York City. *No, sir. I was not serving Viv shrimp that said, this was all I could find in the freezer section, and not I went to the ends of the earth for you.*

As they shifted to the main course, Red watched Viv take her first bite of the succulent and juicy prime rib. Her eyes widened, and she looked at him with pure delight. "This is honestly one of the best prime ribs I've ever had. If you decide to quit your day job, you could be a chef."

Flattered by her praise, Red couldn't help but feel a sense of accomplishment. He also wanted to show Viv he could be diligent and creative outside the bedroom or recording studio. He'd put his heart into preparing a meal that made the night memorable for them both, and it gave him so much pleasure to eat Viv up with his eyes the same way she was devouring her dinner. He had to admit, he just loved watching this woman eat. She savored each bite in the unhurried, deliberate, and appreciative way he had imagined she would savor every touch if they were making love. How someone enjoys food is a good approximation of how they might relish other sensual experiences. If Viv made love anything like she ate, she had to be one hell of a lover. She could eat him up anytime. He couldn't help but imagine what that might be like.

They chatted and laughed between bites and sighs of pleasure and satisfaction. Red's home radiated a warmth, intimacy, and relaxing atmosphere that was only present when Viv was there. He had never seen her so serene, happy, and carefree.

"And now for the *pièce de resistance.*" Red excused himself to the kitchen to prepare the baked Alaska. When he returned with the sweet-smelling mini bonfire in hand, Viv's eyes widened and sparkled with excitement. "I've never had baked Alaska before."

"But you said you wanted it." He'd never been a fan of meringue but fluffed sugary egg whites and vanilla seemed like a minor sacrifice. After all, she was giving up a lot more by staying in Aspen Cove.

"It sounded super fancy and date-worthy. I've seen it only in movies." She laughed. "I guess I did give you a list."

"I'm a man who likes lists and reminders. I try never to leave someone guessing what I want. Makes it harder to be disappointed."

With dinner behind them, Red invited Viv to the sofa. "I thought we could watch a movie together. What do you think?"

Her eyes lit up with enthusiasm. "Sounds perfect. Wow, you are laying on the charm offensive tonight. It seems like the obedience classes with Lucky are rubbing off. Is he as good as you at exercising self-control and not stealing the treats?"

"Oh, he's still much better than me, but I'm learning. Just so you know, I won't be hiding in any cabinets tonight, even if you say 'pineapple.'"

"Don't talk over the characters in the middle of key scenes, and I won't be tempted to resort to desperate measures."

"I hope never to need that safe word again."

Viv laughed, her eyes twinkling with amusement. "It would seem we're past that stage now. Hopefully, she's given up. We made it much harder for her or anyone else to welcome themselves into your home. You're following all the protocols, right? Remember, they keep trouble away from you where it belongs."

"I'm paying attention and doing just as I've been told. Thankfully there's been no one hanging around." That got him thinking about Viv and her job as a bodyguard. She hadn't mentioned what was next. Did she have other upcoming assignments? They hadn't discussed what would happen in the future. Then again, while they'd been together for a while, this was their first official date.

Red thought a romantic comedy was the best bet to keep them focused on the date and maintain some restraint. This movie genre always delivered the feel-good, uproarious laughs and tenderness without hot sex scenes that would have had them ripping off their clothes prematurely. This date was all about extending the anticipation and reveling in it. Their eyes met occasionally, smiles playing on their lips. In one particularly touching scene, Red leaned in and gently kissed Viv's lips. After a few lingering kisses, they pulled apart, both knowing that this sexy tug of war was a key part of the game plan for tonight.

As the movie continued, a pivotal scene unfolded where the heroine faced a difficult choice between her life with the hero and her thriving career.

When the movie ended, Red looked at Viv, curious about her thoughts. "What would you choose?"

"Thankfully, I'm not in that position."

He cocked his head, not understanding. "But you are."

Her eyes widened, realizing the truth in his words. "I guess you're right. But it's not an easy decision, Red. It's a complex situation. What about you? What would you choose?"

Red hesitated, running his fingers through his hair. "I… I don't know. I want to think that love is powerful enough to overcome any obstacle, but it's never that simple, is it?"

Viv sighed, her expression thoughtful. "No, it's not.

And why does it always have to be the woman who has to give up her career and aspirations? Would you give up your career for love?"

"I don't know. I can't imagine my life without music. It's all I know."

"So, if you and I were going to make a go of it, you'd expect me to give up my career?"

He hadn't considered how complex their situation was. "No. It would be easier for you to make adjustments, though?"

Her eyes seemed to glow as if backlit by fire. "Why would you say that?"

Red's face flushed, realizing the implications of his words. "I didn't mean it like that, Viv. I just meant... Well, I don't know what I meant. I guess I hadn't thought it through. We've been so happy right here. I didn't imagine us anywhere else. That's all."

Viv's expression softened slightly, but the fire in her eyes remained. "Red, my career and the business I've helped build is important to me, just like music is important to you. We both worked hard to get where we are. We have invested a lot of ourselves, and other people depend on us too."

He nodded, understanding her point of view, and feeling like the 1950s wanted their idiot back. "You're right. I'm sorry, Viv. That was so stupid of me. I suppose I just got caught up in the idea of us being together and didn't consider the details. But, since we're having this talk now, what if we decide to have a family? I wouldn't want you in danger."

Lucky barked, but they ignored him.

"And I wouldn't want you on the road; that's dangerous

too. What happens with the next Sarah who decides she's the one?"

Red thought they'd be kissing and rolling like thunder by now, but this door had to be opened at some point. It might as well be tonight. Exploring the depths of their desires could wait while they sorted out the depths of their souls. They couldn't live as soulmates if they couldn't figure out how to be together.

Lucky barked louder.

"I think he needs to go out. If you can get him, I'll take care of the dishes that have started to ferment in the sink."

Viv picked up her phone. "Let's go, boy."

CHAPTER TWENTY-ONE

Viv stepped out into the cold fall air, her breath visible as she exhaled. She couldn't shake the unease that settled in her chest after the conversation with Red. It wasn't that she doubted their affection or commitment, but she couldn't help feeling discontented with the idea that one of them would have to change or diminish their career for the other. Both Cameron and Red had said that many things contributed to the demise of their relationship like publicists, social media consultants and managers constantly trying to shape it for their very different fans, but being apart all the time was probably the biggest problem.

As she paced back and forth in front of the house, she considered calling Cameron for advice. But a glance at the time told her it was too late, and maybe Cameron didn't want to be in the middle, providing counsel to her sister-in-law on how to handle the intricacies of a relationship with her ex-fiancé. The crisp air nipped at her uncovered skin, goosebumps rising as she caught a breeze. The scent of fallen leaves and wood smoke hung in the air, reminding her that fall was almost over, and winter wasn't far away. The stillness of the night was only occasionally interrupted by the creaking of swaying tree limbs and the distant hoot of an owl.

Lucky, who had been quietly sniffing the yard's perimeter, suddenly began barking at the gate. Viv furrowed her brow, curious about what had caught the dog's attention.

"What do you hear, boy?" She opened the gate, and Lucky bolted into the patch of trees next to Red's house, his barks growing more frantic.

"Damn it, Lucky!" Viv muttered under her breath, pulling up the flashlight app on her phone. "If you're chasing a cat, I'm going to kill you." The narrow beam cut through the darkness as she ventured into the woods. Her heart pounded. The hairs on the back of her neck stood on end. The rustling of leaves beneath her feet sounded unnaturally loud in the quiet night, and the chill in the air seeped deeper into her bones. She hadn't planned on hiking through the woods when she wore the sleeveless black dress. There was a reason she didn't often dress up. She simply wasn't as comfortable or nimble in a dress as she was with her usual trousers, T-shirt, and jacket.

Moving cautiously in the bejeweled flats, a noise stopped her in her tracks. It was a faint rustling she couldn't pinpoint, but it sounded much larger than a dog of Lucky's size. It would be unusual to have a deer or a bear so close to town, although that kind of thing was happening more and more in areas that were expanding. That didn't apply to Aspen Cove. Stiffening, she aimed her flashlight toward the sound, her grip on the phone tightening as adrenaline coursed through her, knowing something wasn't right. That's when she saw her—Sarah, standing just a few feet away with a handgun pointed directly at her chest.

Viv's heart raced liked a sprinter, her entire body

going rigid as her mind contemplated the fight or flight equation that faced her now. She couldn't outrun a bullet, and neither could Lucky. Staying put was her only choice for now. The light from her phone illuminated Sarah's eerie-looking figure in the woods and then her face, revealing a cold, calculating expression that sent a shiver down Viv's spine. She struggled to find her voice, knowing she needed to act quickly if she hoped to escape this situation.

"Sarah," she finally managed. "What are you doing here?"

Sarah's lips curled into a smile, and her eyes gleamed maliciously. "Oh, Viv," she said, her voice dripping with false sweetness. "I think you know exactly why I'm here."

Viv tried to steady her breathing, her mind speeding through scenarios as she considered her options. If she could stall Sarah long enough, maybe she could find a way to escape or alert Red.

She tried to focus on the weapon but couldn't get a good look at it in the dark. All she saw was a raised hand. "Why don't you put the weapon down, and we can talk about this like adults?" she suggested, trying to sound confident despite the terror that gripped her. She had encountered plenty of danger, but this was her first time confronted with a deranged lunatic pointing a gun at her at close range.

Sarah let out a cold, humorless laugh. "There's no talking our way out of this. Talk? About what? About how you stole Red from me?"

Meanwhile, Lucky bounded forward, and Sarah turned the weapon on him. Viv knew she couldn't just stand there, waiting for the inevitable. So, with a burst of adrenaline, she made her move.

In one swift motion, Viv swung her arm and shifted

forward, aiming the beam of her phone's flashlight directly into Sarah's eyes. Caught off guard, Sarah shielded her face.

Seizing the opportunity, Viv lunged forward, attempting to disarm her attacker.

The two women grappled in the darkness, their desperate struggle accompanied by heavy breathing and the rustling of leaves underfoot. Just as Viv thought she was getting the upper hand, Sarah picked up a rock and hit her on the side of the head.

Viv struggled to regain her bearings; her head spun, and her vision blurred. She knew she couldn't take on Sarah physically, so she had to outsmart her somehow.

As Sarah advanced menacingly toward her, Viv's eyes fell on her phone beside Lucky. With a sudden burst of energy, she lurched for the dog, grabbing her phone in the process. She pulled them both to her chest, hoping Sarah wouldn't notice that she now had her phone.

A sharp pain lanced through her head, and she reached up to touch the egg that had formed where Sarah had hit her.

"Just let us go," she said.

"So you can go back inside and play house with my Red? I don't think so. Get to your feet," she demanded.

With her heart pounding, Viv complied, her legs feeling like jelly beneath her. Sarah ordered her through the trees, and when they emerged, she gestured to a nearby car, her weapon never wavering from Viv's direction. "Get in," she ordered.

As Viv climbed into the passenger seat, Sarah took the driver's position and started the car, peeling away from their location. Sarah drove out of town, took a right at the highway, and they were plunged deeper into the dark woods, the headlights casting ghostlike shadows on the trees as they sped past. The forest, which had always felt like Viv's protector, suddenly felt as scary as Sarah. Viv turned to her instincts and her training, trying to come up with a plan while her head spun, and the ghostly shadows in the trees darted in and out of view. She kept her phone close to her chest. It was her lifeline, and she'd use it at the first opportunity.

After what felt like an eternity but was probably no more than an hour, Sarah pulled the car to a stop in a clearing, far from any sign of civilization. "End of the road for you; get out."

Viv, feeling more vulnerable than ever, did as she was told. It was the only choice under the circumstances. She stepped out of the car and into the chilly night air. Lucky burrowed against her. She wasn't sure if he was seeking warmth or safety. At this point, she couldn't provide either. How did she, a bodyguard, get into a situation like this? She thought Sarah was a nut and a nuisance but not a killer. Were her instincts really that far off? Her only conclusion was that she was terrible at her job. She had gotten distracted thinking about Red and let her guard down. There must have been something she missed. If she got out of this, she was quitting and working as a local barista. At least there, she wouldn't be faced with life-or-death matters. Then she thought about how close to committing murder she could come when faced with a lack of caffeine.

As she stood there, waiting for whatever Sarah had planned for her, Viv summoned the courage to ask, "Are you going to kill me?"

Sarah threw her head back and laughed, her voice now light and airy, a stark contrast to their threatening situation and her psycho intonation in the woods. "Oh, Viv, don't be so dramatic. I'm a lover, not a fighter. I don't know what spell you put on him, but I need to break it. I'm just doing what I know Red wants me to, so that he can be with me. He's going to stop playing hard to get." Sarah's voice returned to its icy tone. "It will take you a long time to find your way out of here. Kill you? What for? Of course, it would be a shame if the bears get you." She then stared at the weapon in her hand and giggled. "It's not even loaded."

As soon as she heard that, Viv rushed forward, but Sarah jumped into the car and sped away, leaving her in the dark.

Once alone, Viv hid at the edge of the tree line and tried to dial Red, but she had no connectivity, so she used the flashlight to illuminate her way down the semblance of a dirt road. She was really in the woods. It took her nearly an hour to get to a place where she had a single bar, and as soon as she did, she knew she was already too late to let Red know that Sarah was on her way. Given Sarah's actions and erratic behavior, she knew Red was in danger. He would never play along with Sarah's delusion. There was a saying, "Hell hath no fury like a woman scorned." And since Red had rejected Sarah once, there was no telling what she'd do when he did it again.

Viv immediately dialed the sheriff.

"Sheriff Cooper," he answered.

"It's Red. He's in trouble."

"Viv, is that you?"

She quickly explained her situation, and how she was now stuck in the forest.

"What can you see around you?"

"Don't think about me. Think of Red." A single flicker shone from her phone, then it died.

CHAPTER TWENTY-TWO

Red couldn't believe Viv had stormed off, taking Lucky with her. As he replayed their conversation, he realized he would gladly give up his career for her if it meant they could be together. But, would it really come to that? Two dedicated and creative people could surely come up with a plan.

He quickly dismissed the thought of calling Val. He remembered Val's stern warning about making Viv unhappy and using him for target practice if he did. Val hadn't seemed like he was joking.

Feeling lost, Red grabbed his keys and climbed into the truck. He knew Viv could be stubborn and might prefer walking all the way back home to Val's rather than asking for a ride, but it was cold, and she wasn't dressed for this weather or a nighttime hike. The quiet streets were dark and silent. The tension of their earlier exchange weighed heavily on him, his heart aching with every passing minute. And then he began to worry. Where would she have gone in the cool night with only a sleeveless dress and a dog?

A nagging thought crept into Red's mind: everyone always seemed to leave him eventually. At least the only people he cared about had. Those in it only for a good time would have stayed forever. The painful realization that he might have driven her away made him even more desperate to find Viv and make amends for his stupidity. Their relationship and her love meant everything to him. Viv had become the air he breathed. He needed to stop thinking of himself and make things right with her.

In a last-ditch effort to locate Viv, he stopped by Bishop's Brewhouse thinking she'd perhaps walked there to get a ride from Jackson. He entered, but only Doc sat at the bar. Next to him was a napkin with a game of tic-tac-toe. He was nursing the beer he'd won.

"Hey, Doc."

"Are you here for more therapy? You look like someone stole your puppy."

Red's eyes widened. If Doc only knew how close he was. "I could use some advice, but I'm in a hurry."

Doc slugged his beer down. "And I could use another." He slid his mug to the edge. "Jackson!"

Jackson emerged from the back room. He looked at Doc's empty mug and then at Red. "You buying?"

Red pulled a ten from his wallet and took a seat. "Just for him."

Jackson poured Doc another and disappeared once again.

"Listen here, son, we need to make this quick anyway. Lovey likes lights out by eleven. What's on your mind?"

"We argued, and she stormed off with Lucky."

Doc looked up from his drink, his eyes lighting up. "I was only joking about the dog."

"I'm not. Viv's been gone for nearly an hour, and I don't know what to do. I called her phone, but she's not picking up. Now it seems like she shut it off. I drove around looking for her, but she wasn't anywhere to be found. What do I do?"

"Give her some time, son. If she walked away, then she needed space. It's never a good idea to chase down an argument. Go home, sleep on it, and you two can figure it out in the morning."

He knew Doc was right about chasing the argument, but the thought of Viv out there, unhappy, made it difficult for him to walk away. Despite Doc's advice, Red continued searching for her, desperate to make things right and prove that he was different—that he wouldn't let her walk out of his life. He was also worried about her but knew she was very resourceful and would have called Val to get her if necessary. Red calling Val would only inflame things.

When it became clear that he wouldn't find her and every call went to voice mail, he went home and got ready for bed. The faster he fell asleep, the quicker he'd see her again. As he drifted off, his mind played out how very different he thought this night would be.

Sometime later, a cool hand rested on his chest and slipped down his stomach.

"You came back," he said groggily. Against his better judgement, he left the door unlocked and the alarm unarmed just in case, but for once it worked in his favor. "I'm so sorry." He rolled over and pulled her into his arms. Everything was wrong, from the feel of her skin to the smell of her perfume. Viv never wore perfume; she smelled like sunshine and flowers and happiness without it. The woman beside him smelled like stale cigarettes, whiskey, and desperation.

"It's okay, love; I got back in. We have some time."

He flew out of bed, pulled on his jeans from the chair

beside the bed before he flipped the switch to turn the light on, and found Sarah naked and in his bed.

"You? How the hell did you get in here again? Where's Viv?"

She laid back and rolled her eyes. "I left her in the woods. You should be happy. I got rid of what was getting in our way."

Panic ripped through him, and strangely enough, it was quickly followed by a sense of relief too. Viv hadn't left him, despite the evidence to the contrary. He rushed toward Sarah, ready to extract the truth from her by whatever means necessary, when suddenly, a loud noise came from the front door. Sheriff Cooper stormed in with his gun drawn and a look on his face that could cut right through steel.

Within minutes, the sheriff had Sarah dressed, cuffed, and in his cruiser.

"I'm going to look for Viv," Red said.

The sheriff shook his head. "I don't need two of you lost in the woods. I'll get a search party together. Follow me to the station."

There was no way Red was waiting another minute to find her. He jumped in his truck and looked like he was following the sheriff, but when the sheriff turned toward town, Red headed toward the mountains. Sarah said she left Viv in the woods.

He knew that he had to stop panicking and start thinking like Viv if he wanted to find her. Viv had always said that fear could cloud your judgment—the worst thing you can do is panic when in danger. He took a moment and examined the facts: she was in the woods, she had a phone, but it stopped working, or perhaps the connection got lost. His mind was doing calisthenics, imagining a thousand scenarios, from animal encounters to Viv getting hurt because of her fancy clothes and impractical shoes. Was Lucky still with her? Had Sarah hurt either of them?

The moment the thought of the dog entered his mind, he knew Viv was right. It was time to look at the facts and devise a plan. Lucky was wearing his collar—the one with the Apple AirTag. He had bought it on a whim, and Viv had made fun of him for it. Now, this silly purchase might be the only thing to save her and Lucky. He pulled out his phone and opened the Find My app. Lucky's location showed up as soon as he clicked on the tag. It was moving. That had to be a good sign—unless he and Viv had been separated and he was now lost in the woods on his own. Red had to go with what he had—a signal. A signal that was a lifeline to the woman he loved and the pet who had also stolen his heart and made them a family of sorts. He was fighting for his family, the family he was building now. Hitting the gas pedal to its max capacity, he raced up the highway and onto a logging trail. Part of his suspension and transmission were probably left behind in that mad dash. The truck rocked over the makeshift road, nearly tipping at least once over the twenty miles or so he forged into the forest, leaving clouds of dust in his wake. Out of the shadows he could almost make out a figure in the distance and swung sideways, so his headlights illuminated the area, the dust creating another large cloud behind him. There in front of him stood Viv, hugging Lucky close to her chest.

When she realized through the dust cloud and bright headlights that it was him, she smiled, and tears streamed across her face. She ran to him and collapsed in his arms, burying her face in his chest.

"Oh, thank God you're okay," she said. "I'm so sorry I failed you. How did I miss how psychotic and dangerous

Sarah was? When she didn't come around, I thought she'd given up. I let my guard, and you, down. I'm a terrible bodyguard."

He took off his jacket and covered her bare shoulders, placing his arms back around her.

"Viv, it's not your fault. You only took Lucky out and couldn't have known what would happen. I thought she was gone too." He pressed his lips to the top of her head. "You didn't fail me. In fact, because of your quick thinking and calling the sheriff, I'm safe now. And the only reason I found you was because your voice was in my head. I didn't let fear rule me." He held on to her so tightly he was afraid he'd crush her. "Well, I did at first. I thought you left me."

"Left you? Why would I leave you?"

"Because you thought I was asking you to give it all up."

She sighed and pressed herself closer to him. "Everything worth having is worth fighting for, especially you."

"I'd never ask you to give up what you love for me. Let's not invent ways to break up when all we both want is to be together. There is no problem we can't work through if we do it together, Viv. We deserve the love we can build. We deserve this life together and we can make it whatever we want." He rubbed her arms, trying to get some heat back into them. "Look at you, you have to be freezing still. Let's get you some more heat." He walked them to the parked truck and helped her inside before dashing around the front to his side.

Before climbing inside, he messaged the sheriff to tell him Viv was safe. When he closed the door, she said, "You thought I left you and took your dog?"

"Our dog." He hung his head. "I've never had someone I wanted stay."

She scooted over until she was seated next to him. "I'm

not going anywhere. How crazy would that be? You make me eggs in the morning and prime rib for dinner. I'd comment on your bedroom skills, but I haven't experienced those yet."

He put the truck in gear. "I feel with the right inspiration, I can really cook in the bedroom, too."

CHAPTER TWENTY-THREE

All Viv wanted when they got home was to climb into Red's bed and experience the carnal closeness they had been building up to for weeks, not to mention the hours of pleasantly torturous anticipation baked into their first date. Instead, she got a living room full of people—Val, Doc, and several others from town who had heard about her being spirited away by a psycho fan of Red's. She was grateful for their concern, but right now, all she wanted was some privacy and time alone with Red. She had never imagined herself a damsel in distress, but she had to admit there was something pretty darn sexy about Red showing up on his steel horse. She had taught him well after all.

As soon as they walked through the door, Doc approached her, concern written all over his face. "Viv, let me look at that head of yours."

Viv sighed but allowed Doc to examine her nasty bump. She winced as he gently prodded the area where Sarah had hit her with the rock. "It doesn't look too bad, but you should take it easy for a few days," he advised as he continued his examination. "I don't see any signs of concussion, but head injuries can evolve. You call me at the first sign of new pain, nausea, blurred vision. Tell Red he needs to call an ambulance if there is any loss of consciousness." Red reappeared. She hadn't seen him for a few minutes.

"Yes, Doc. Really, I'm fine, but we will pay attention." She wasn't thinking of the lump on her head but rather how quickly she could get Red out of his jeans. *Geez, when will everyone leave us alone?*

Meanwhile, Val approached Red, his expression serious. "Thanks for coming to my sister's rescue. I can't tell you how much it means to me, even if it was your crazy-ass fan who wanted to hurt her."

Red, holding Lucky, offered a nod. "I'm just glad we found her. She's tough, though; she handled the situation well, but I guess you would have expected that already."

Viv rolled her eyes, but secretly, she was pleased by Red's praise. She wished she could bask in the warmth of his words, but the room was still full of concerned faces.

Eventually, everyone filtered out of the house, leaving Viv, Red, and Lucky alone. She moved closer to Red, wrapping her arms around him. "Thank you," she whispered.

He hugged her tightly, resting his chin on her head. "You don't have to thank me, Viv. I would have walked across fire for you. That's what you do when you love someone."

She knew the words weren't easy for him. They came with so much risk. To love someone meant you had to open up the most vulnerable part of your being and let them in. She didn't take his words lightly.

Viv looked up at him, her eyes shimmering with tears she could hold back no more. "I love you too." She swiped the tears from her cheeks and smiled. "I didn't want to wear one of those AirTags, but maybe we should rethink that. You know, just in case."

Red chuckled, kissing her forehead. "I can't lose you if I never let you out of my sight."

As they stood there, wrapped in each other's arms, Viv knew that despite the ordeal she'd just experienced, she had never felt more secure.

Red's house was a place that had begun to feel like home. The familiar scent of his cologne and that old guitar in the corner filled her with a sense of comfort and belonging.

"Let me put you to bed. Doc said you should take it easy for a few days."

"You can take me to bed, but I'll be disappointed if you take it too easy on me."

Their eyes met, and seeing the hunger in his caused her heart to skip a beat. "Are you sure?" He gently brushed her cheek with the back of his fingers, the warmth of his touch sending shivers of bliss through her.

She closed her eyes momentarily, savoring the feeling and the emotions it stirred within her. "Absolutely positive."

Their lips met in a tender and deliberate kiss, a sweet taste of love and trust. Their hands danced, exploring one another's bodies, and Viv marveled at the sensations coursing through her. The feel of Red's strong hands on her skin, the sound of their breathing, and the heat of their connection were intoxicating.

He led her to his room, and the bath filled with red rose petals he had prepared earlier as the last gate of anticipation to cross before what he knew would follow. Viv guessed he must have filled it with water while Doc was finishing his exam. She wondered where he had gone. The fragrance of the rose petals in the hot water rose to her nostrils and made the air sensual and inviting. They undressed one another; Red pulled the single zipper on Viv's dress and let it fall to the floor. His hands and gravity dispatched Viv's bra and underwear next. Viv could tell by Red's expression and the change in his body temperature that he liked what he saw. Their movements were unhurried and deliberate, a silent promise that they had all the time in the world. As they climbed into the bath, their bodies entwined, Viv reveled in the warmth of the water and Red's body pressed against hers. When her fingers pruned, she said, "Let's get out." She wanted the full landscape of Red's bed for what would follow.

At first, they kissed with a pace and tenderness that belied the urgency of their need.

Running his hands along the curve of her body, he adored every inch of her. His eyes feasted upon her, and his fingers sought to memorize each inch of her curves and planes. Viv felt her skin flush as he brushed his lips across her flesh.

Their breathing joined in a synchronized chorus of panting, echoing the rhythm of their hearts beating in perfect time. He spent what felt like a lifetime tantalizing and tormenting her, but when he entered her, it was tender and transcendent. People often said the best things are worth waiting for, but she was glad she hadn't delayed another minute.

"That was unbelievable," she sighed.

"No, Viv. That was only the beginning." Red took Viv to heights of pleasure she never knew existed as she felt him love her again with everything he had.

As they lay together afterward, their limbs tangled and their breaths mingling, Viv rested her head on Red's chest, listening to the steady rhythm of his heart. It was a soothing sound, a reminder that they were alive and together.

As Red's fingers traced idle patterns on her skin, he whispered sweet words into her hair. "I love you, Viv. I can't imagine my life without you."

Tears pricked at the corners of her eyes, but she blinked them back. "I love you too, Red. You'll never have to imagine that because I can't be without you."

Viv couldn't help but feel a profound sense of contentment as they drifted off to sleep. She was exactly where she was meant to be, wrapped in Red's arms. The world outside, with all its dangers and uncertainty, seemed to fade away, leaving them in their cocoon of warmth and safety.

She glanced at the corner where one of Red's guitars sat, a silent witness to their love, and she smiled. Their passion which had filled the room lingered still, and she couldn't help but wonder if it would inspire him to create beautiful melodies about their journey together.

As sleep finally claimed her, Viv knew deep in her heart that their love was strong enough to overcome any obstacle.

CHAPTER TWENTY-FOUR

Viv sat on the couch in Red's boxer shorts and T-shirt, and he'd never seen her look so beautiful. The last few weeks were spent making love or eating—or both. He was happy to say that Viv's appetite in the bedroom was just as ravenous as it was in the kitchen. She never seemed to get her fill, and he was thrilled to oblige her every craving.

They'd settled into a happy routine. Viv stayed with Vortex as the CEO but ran it from a spare room in Red's house in Aspen Cove. She would no longer leave on assignment but run the cybersecurity end of things. Red decided he was no longer touring. His favorite place was sitting in his living room, playing guitar, and watching Viv rule over Vortex. She could do anything she put her mind to, but he loved that she chose the path that would keep her there with him.

Red grabbed his guitar and sat beside her, a playful glint in his eyes. "I've written you a song."

"Do you think that's wise? I mean, you could be singing it for the rest of your life," she said, gently mocking what he had told her months ago.

"I hope so."

He began to strum the chords. *Oh, Viv, my love, you light up my day. But there's something funny, I just have to say, When you dance in the kitchen, it's a sight to see. Your moves are wild, but they're perfect to me.*

You're my quirky girl, my lovable goof. Together we're solid. We're bulletproof.

You wear mismatched socks. It's your signature style. But baby, you pull it off with grace and a smile. And when you sing. You're slightly off-key. But that's what makes it charming to me.

You're my quirky girl, my lovable goof. Together, we're solid. we're bulletproof.

His voice filled the room as he sang the humorous lyrics.

Viv's eyes widened in surprise, but soon she was chuckling and shaking her head in disbelief.

As Red finished the song, Viv laughed out loud. "That's my love sonnet? A song where you pick on my dancing and pitch problems? You missed that I eat a lot."

He did his best to look serious. "You don't like it? I thought the band could play it at our wedding. I figured Lucky could be our flower dog." He sat across from her, doing his best to look earnest, and it appeared as if it was working, until she smiled, and he broke out into laughter.

"Oh my gosh. This is your payback for me pineappleing you."

"I said I'd get you back."

Viv leaned in, pressing a soft kiss to his lips. "You got me good." She lifted her brows as if it had finally dawned on her that he was talking about their wedding. "Wedding? Flower dog?"

He situated his guitar and began to strum the chords again. He'd been writing this song for her since the moment he met her. It originally played in his head and now played from his heart.

From the moment I saw you, my world turned anew, a spark in your eyes, like the sunrise, so true. We danced through the days like a sweet serenade; through laughter and tears, our love never fades.

You're my heart, you're my soul, you're the melody; together, we've grown in perfect harmony.

The nights we've spent under a sky full of stars. We've shared our dreams, our hopes, and our scars. Your touch sets me ablaze. Our love intertwines. With every beat of your heart, I know that you're mine.

He looked into her eyes for the next verse.

And now I stand before you, my heart in my hand. With a question that lingers like prints in the sand. For a love that's unyielding, a love that's so true. I can't imagine a life without you. So, Viv, my love, my laughter, my muse. I stand here before you, hoping it's me that you choose. Will you marry me and share this beautiful ride. Let's walk hand in hand, and side by side.

He set down his guitar, took a knee, and drew a Tiffany box from his pocket. The only time he remembered being this nervous was when he stepped on the stage, hoping the audience would love him. And now, none of that mattered because a life without Vivian Armstrong wasn't a life worth living.

"You're asking me to marry you?"

He smiled. "Well, I'm not asking Lucky."

"That's good because he's not really your type; he's got bad breath, and he licks himself."

She opened the box and saw the ring he'd chosen for her. It was two bands twisted together without an end. In the center was a solitaire that glistened and sparkled. Viv's eyes welled up with tears as she looked back up at Red and nodded, her voice trembling. "This is ... beautiful," she whispered.

"It pales in comparison to you." Red took her hand and slipped the ring onto her finger. It fit perfectly, just like the two of them, destined to be woven together forever.

"Viv, you make me the happiest man alive," he said, his voice thick with emotion. "I promise to spend the rest of my life working to make you just as happy."

She laughed. "You better because I'm a damn good shot."

He'd almost forgotten that he would become a target if she ever became unhappy, but that would never be an issue. He'd spend the rest of his life making sure of it.

"Yes, I will marry you—and Lucky."

They sealed their promise with a tender, passionate kiss, and as they held each other close, they knew they had found happily ever after in each other's arms.

Thank You for Reading *One Hundred Desires*!

I hope you enjoyed Aspen Cove and the heartwarming story of Vivian and Red. The romance continues with *One Hundred Merry Memories*! Scan the QR code below to get your copy of *One Hundred Merry Memories* and follow Amanda and Jackson's journey!

ONE HUNDRED DESIRES

OTHER BOOKS BY KELLY COLLINS

Dive into heartwarming romance, unforgettable love stories, and second chances. Explore all of Kelly Collins' series and find your next favorite happily-ever-after! 💘

Recipes for Love

A Taste of Temptation

A Pinch of Passion

A Dash of Desire

A Cup of Compassion

A Dollop of Delight

A Layer of Love

Recipe for Love Collection 1-3

Recipe for Love Collection 4-6

The Second Chance Series

Set Free

Set Aside

Set in Stone

Set Up

Set on You

The Second Chance Series Box Set

A Pure Decadence Series

Yours to Have

Yours to Conquer

Yours to Protect

A Pure Decadence Collection

Wilde Love Series

Betting On Him

Betting On Her

Betting On Us

A Wilde Love Collection

The Boys of Fury Series

Redeeming Ryker

Saving Silas

Delivering Decker

The Boys of Fury Boxset

Making the Grade Series

The Dean's List

Honor Roll

The Learning Curve

Making the Grade Box Set

Stand Alone Billionaire Novels

Dream Maker

GET A FREE BOOK.

Go to www.authorkellycollins.com

ABOUT THE AUTHOR

International bestselling author of over 50 novels, Kelly Collins crafts stories that keep love alive. With a heart full of romance and a vivid imagination, she blends real-life events into captivating tales that contemporary romance, new adult, and romantic suspense fans will fall for over and over again.

For More Information
www.authorkellycollins.com
kelly@authorkellycollins.com

Printed in Great Britain
by Amazon